Gay Erotica Mega Bundle

Davie Dix

Published by Tales of Flesh Press, 2014.

GAY EROTICA MEGA BUNDLE

First edition. July 27, 2014.

Copyright © 2014 Davie Dix.

ISBN: 979-8201930479

Written by Davie Dix.

Man Meat At The Movies

(His Big Fat Sausage)

"Jim, I want to suck you dry while we're sitting in a movie theatre," Ben declared.

I nearly sputtered my coffee all over the table, and looked over in amazement at his wide eyed eagerness. It wasn't what he said which floored me, but it was the fact he did it so loudly, and on the crowded patio of the little restaurant we were meeting at.

"Well then," I said, after regaining my composure. "How else are two handsome lads like us suppose to spend an afternoon?"

Our smiles reflected in each others big stylish sunglasses. Just two hot dudes in mutual dick sucking agreement.

Glad I asked him out for coffee.

"And I want you to suck me off, as well," he said with a wry grin. "It's only fair." He sipped at his cup, making a point to suck on it noisily, and with gusto.

I tingled at the sound. Actually, one particularly sensitive appendage tingled the most. Perhaps it was in anticipation?

It's not everyday I pick up a piece of ass like Ben. Certainly not after we fought over the same pair of shoes at a sale, just the other day. It would seem this guy has good taste and I was confident it would be in more ways than one.

"Is this a fantasy of yours?" I asked. I noticed out of the corner of my eye, two girls at another table had taken a keen interest in our loud, and boisterous fellatio talk. Who could blame them?

"Sucking your cock?"

I laughed. "No, your cock. Being sucked. In a theatre." I crooked an eyebrow at the two girls. Neither one seemed to know what to do with themselves in such a situation. I turned away, dismissing them from my mind and potential conquests.

Too bad. A creative foursome would have certainly topped off my day. Ah well.

Ben didn't seem to notice the others, or perhaps just didn't care, either. Major points awarded to him for that. "No," he said. "But it is now." Again with the coffee slurping.

Point taken.

We eyed each other hungrily; respective clothing imaginatively being removed via horny imagination. Not to be outdone, I slurped on my coffee, too.

He shuddered. His broad shoulders heaved as only broad shoulders could. I imagined what his nipples were like; color, size, taste. My mouth started to water at the thought of them in my mouth, suckling like a new born babe. Warm, firm muscular flesh enveloping my lips, pressing against my chin, nose buried.

"That could be arranged," I said, waggling my eyebrows over my stylish shades at him. Nothing quite beats talking about sex to get your juices going. Other than *actual* romping, of course.

Anxious to get this horny show on the road, I stood up. "Shall we?"

Ben followed suit. "You bet!"

As I turned to leave one of the girls was stupid enough to ask, "Could my friend and I join you? We'd like the company of two hunks such as yourselves."

Was this chick for real?

"Are you for real?" I blurted. The smile fell from his face, and Ben and I marched by, noses in the air.

We bantered at the register over who was going to pay. I let him win. Then we headed out and onto the street, with the noon day sun bringing out the smiles on our faces.

I noticed we had some people in our glorious wake.

I leaned over to Ben and whispered in his ear, "Hopeless girls are hopeless."

Ben looked back and saw those two girls following behind.

"Think they'll get the point?"

"They're women, of course they won't. It would take divine intervention to close those gaping vaginas from wanting to be bad."

Suddenly, their boyfriends arrived, adorning scowls on their faces once they saw us.

"Busted!" I shouted. We laughed and practically skipped away.

We arrived outside the theatre and made a feeble attempt at looking interested when scanning the showings. We both had another type of entertainment on our dirty little minds.

"What do you want to see?" he said, playing coy.

"Does it matter?" I said. "Preferably very loud with a lot of dark moments."

We bought a pair of tickets to the closest showing for whatever was available. Couldn't tell you what it was. I'm sure it was good. Oscar winner, perhaps. I just didn't care one bit.

The carpeting inside looked as if all the left over neon orange and purple coloring in the world came there to die. There were clots of annoying people everywhere, none of whom were as remotely interesting and sexy as Ben and I.

A light bulb flickered over my said dirty mind.

"Let's have some fun while we wait," I said, steering him towards the handicapped washroom door.

I glanced around to see if we were being observed, and shockingly, we weren't. (I know! What a shock.) I unceremoniously shoved him inside and locked the door. The bathroom had a single toilet, single sink and lots of room.

Perfect for what I had in mind.

I pointed at the sink's counter. "Drop those pants and get up on there. Time for a little pre-movie snack."

His eyes went wide with excitement, but his expression was immediately replaced with concern. "What if someone finds us in here?"

I raised an eyebrow. "We could only hope! Now get your slutty self up there or I'll give you a spanking!" And with that I reached around him and smacked his rump really hard. The fleshy sound it made was amplified by the tacky purple tiling which encased this toilet/sex nook.

"Ow!" he squealed, but it was mostly for show.

As he dropped his pants and turned to navigate the mighty sheer face of Mount Sink, I smacked his ass again. With such a solid caboose, it barely moved. I felt my mouth water.

Needless to say, he didn't wear any underwear, not even the string variety. Easy access, just the way I like it.

His wonderful cock dangled from a crotch completely barren of hair, smooth to the touch, and just yearning to be licked and played with. He was all bare flesh.

Can't have too much hair in that area, could be a choking hazard.

I ignored all preamble and immediately secured my mouth to his prick, which was already getting swollen. Reaching behind his thighs I pulled myself closer to him, making certain he wouldn't escape my tongue gymnastics. Not that he would, but I can get intense sometimes.

I vacuumed his head between my lips, sucking hard. My tongue constantly wiggled against it. God, do I love me some dick! I sucked and teased his flesh with my tongue and lips for quite a while, occasionally engulfing it with my hot mouth. He started to shudder with pleasurable intensity.

Not wanting him to pop just yet, I eased off to just licking. Nice and long, up and down the entire length of his shaft. Occasionally, I included a tongue flick on his pretty little ass-hole (he bleaches, too! Damn this guy is a keeper) which caused him to gasp each time in surprise.

Then I stopped, only to resume my assault with a full finger. In and out, and all around, using my free thumb to rub around his now puckering ass-hole. Gotta use the thumb for something.

As I worked my fingers up and down, listening to the succulent squish – squish noises it coaxed from spit-wet fuckhole, my eyes ran over his naked flesh.

Head tilted back resting against the mirror, eyes closed, mouth open and panting with growing intensity, I could tell I had him exactly where I wanted him.

Slowly, I withdrew my finger from him. It was slick with his ass sweat. Locking eyes with him I opened my mouth wide, put it all the way inside, as if to gag myself, and closed my lips around it. Then, while making a sumptuous 'mmmm' noise, I slid it out of my mouth, sucking up over little bit of him.

I leaned forward and put that finger in his mouth, and he started to suck on it as well. While he was distracted I jammed a couple of the fingers of my free hand inside his ass again, roughly. He moaned, but kept working my finger. I could feel his hot tongue against it.

I am an ambidextrous finger banger.

Not quite satisfied I was done, I resume sucking his massive dong, taking it as far into my throat until his nut sack was firmly pressed against my chin. I started to count to ten. Maybe I could break my previous record.

Someone knocked on the door. My face was too full of wondrous cock and balls to do anything about it.

They knocked louder. Each rap had a more insistent tone. Perhaps they wanted some attention, or something?

I don't know about your fellatio skills, but it's pretty damn hard to deep throat a cock, particularly the massive kind, and concentrate on what your doing, when another person is practically kicking a door in which is a couple feet from your head.

They kept knocking.

Gasping, Ben said, "Hate to end this so soon, but I think someone really needs to use the crapper."

I stopped, carefully withdrew his meat from my throat, then mouth. I gently withdrew my fingers from his ass, too. Gasping for air I still managed to pout in disappointment.

"Okay," I said, giving his slick dick one last lick. "To be continued."

We each stood and Ben put on his pants while I washed ass juice from my mouth and chin. Still, whomever it was kept knocking.

After a few minutes, we were satisfied with our looks and then we opened the door.

A cute guy was standing outside with an much older man holding a cane, obviously his father. They had been the ones knocking on the door.

I hoped no one would think anything about two hot guys, glazed with sweat, exiting a bathroom together. But as we passed by I made sure to catch the younger guy's gaze and flashed some very obvious bedroom eyes at him.

His eyes, widen, too, but in shock. His mouth dropped open a little and an electric thrill went threw me. Hmmm. Never did a father-son team before. Rare for me to have any firsts left on my list of things to do before I die.

As the cute guy guided his oblivious father towards the can, I made a point of suddenly smacking Ben's ass and gripping a buttock, who suppressed a squeal.

The son paused and stared in amazement. I gave him a wink and Ben and I were back on our way to our next little thrill in the theatre.

Suddenly, an angry little Vietnamese man marched up to us. I recognized him instantly. It was the manager. He scowled at us, centring his attention onto me.

"You again!" he cried.

I dropped him a wink. "Yup," I said. "Aren't you a lucky little troll to have my infrequent patronage?" I waved our tickets at him. "Paying customer, always good."

"No dirty," he said, shaking a finger at me. What was this with fingers today? I was actually starting to feel he was teasing me with it. He did appear to have a good technique.

"No worries sweetie, we'll be discrete." I steered us away.

Ben gave me a questioning look. "You've been here before?" he asked with a humorous tone.

I made a show of looking around and noticing the place for the first time. "Gee, I don't know. I do get around a lot. Could be I graced this dump with my sexy presence before."

He laughed and squeezed my hand. "Making friends wherever you go, huh? I'm impressed. Well let's make sure they remember me, okay?" The devilish expression on his face made me want to take him right then and there on the crummy purple and red colored carpet of the theatre lobby. Now wouldn't that make for an interesting tale? Maybe the next one.

Hand in hand, we entered the theatre proper. Only a handful of people were seated, mostly in the middle seats. All eyes turned to us and I couldn't help but grin at their attention. I mean, really, how could you not ogle two horny hot fags holding hands? (Say that ten times real quick.)

"Where should we fu-," he started to say but stopped himself with a sheepish grin. "I mean where should we sit?"

I laughed and pulled him along the aisle.

We picked the most conspicuous location that people who fuck in theatres try and hide themselves: the far back corner.

We settled in, all the while making little effort to ignore the attention we were getting.

Once the theatre darkened, and the trailers began, Ben attacked, undoing the buttons on my shirt, while quietly kissing me.

Out popped pectoral number one, which he immediately seized and gently squeezed. He rubbed my nipple with his thumb and pinched it occasionally. Then he sucked on it like a starving infant.

Out popped pectoral number two. For the longest time, that one got most of his hungry attention. But he alternated between the two, making my nipples, and the hot skin around them, slick with his spit. They glistened in the murky darkness of the theatre, and practically sparkled when the movie had brighter scenes.

Sucking, licking, pinching, gasping, quiet moaning, slurping all adds up to a pleasant movie going experience. I'd highly recommend it.

Fuck, he was making me hard.

I grabbed one of his hands and eased it down between my bulging crotch.

He released my nipple from his mouth with a pop, and stuck his tongue out a little to one side as he made a show of concentrating on navigating my nether regions with his fingers.

He had no problem there. He was an expert guide in this area, no doubt reconnoitring other similar trails with similarly eager guys. He was a Sherpa-guide for the most hard of dicks.

Out popped my cock, and the sudden motion caused a moan from me.

He leaned in close to my ear and said, "Well, someone made that easy for me. It's like your body was just waiting from me to violate it in that way." He sucked in my earlobe, and teethed it gently, all the while stoking me with a hand (was it two hands now?) up and down my shaft of hard blue steel.

Sorry to be crude, but that really does describe my dick at that point:

Hard.

Blue.

Steel.

Get over it. Or get a grip, like him.

Ben suckled my earlobe, teething it and flicking it with his hot tongue. His fingers eased up and down, slow and easy at first. But soon his movements became more frantic.

He jerked me like that for long, wondrous minutes. I have no clue how long, lost in the nirvana that was his expert touch.

At one point, during a very quiet part of the movie, the theatre was almost silent. And all I could hear was the muted sounds of a hand vigorously stroking a cock.

Guess that was mine!

Yet, so entranced with what was unfolding on the screen, none of the other movie goers were even remotely aware of my unfolding at the back of the room.

Then, Ben got out of his seat and eased himself in front of me. Not a lot of room between my goods and the chair in front of me, but his close proximity excited me even more. Then he knelt down as best as he could, getting down and under my pants which were at my knees.

He pushed against the inside of my calves, exposing all my bare ass for the world to behold. The armrests of my chair at first limited my spread, but I wiggled my bum down a bit and I was able to get my knees nearly up next to my ears. I firmly put my feet against the headrest of the chair in front of me, horny, hungry faggot trapped between them.

I interlocked my fingers behind his head and pressed his face deep against me, even going so far as to grind my hips around as much as the seat would allow. He said, "Mmmmmm. Mmmmm. Mmmmm." Or words to the effect. Hard to make out what is being said with a face full of ass. Holding onto his head, I eased the pressure and he took a few moments to gasp for air. Then I suddenly shoved his face into my ass again. "Mmmmm. Mmmmm. Mmmmm." Three, two, one. Released. Gasp gasp. Shove.

I did this to him several times, over and over.

Ben looked up, lifted his mouth above my nut sack, and whispered, "God, do I love me some shaved ass!" He resumed licking my hole, like a good little man-bitch.

I chuckled. "It's not like I can't handle hairy ass, it's just that when it resembles a thatch roof after a monsoon, even a professional rimmer like myself has gotta say no."

I enjoyed the sensation of his giggling motion had against the inner portion of my butt cheeks.

I finally released him, and he breathed heavily, his chest heaving with the effort. I could see by the dim light that his mouth and chin were wet with spittle and sweat. I leaned forward, grabbing his head and pulling it towards me.

We kissed, passionately. Tongue wrestling with the best of them. I could taste myself on him, all over him. I ran my tongue over his chin, kissing my on ass from him.

We did this for more long moments, until I had licked his face clean of my own sweet essence (and Dear God do I taste good, if I do say so myself!).

Then I looked him in the eyes. "Suck on my dick, bitch," I whispered. He was happy to oblige. He worked my prick like an old pro. The sensation of his tongue and the sucking of his mouth causing me to shudder and writhe. Sweet Lordy that dude's gotta mouth on him!

Head tilted back in pleasure, licking my lips and firmly affixing his face to my cock with my hands at the back of his skull, I actually opened my eyes and looked at the movie screen.

The lead actor was doing it with the lead actress! Playful camera angles, and well placed shadows hid their full nudity, which was no doubt an iron clad clause in each of their contracts. I glanced down at Ben as he hungrily sucked and licked with gusto. I chuckled. No contracts needed here!

I caught movement out of the corner of my eye to the left. Glancing over I saw two men several seats over, and one row down. I as the theatre lit up a bit I recognized them.

It was the guy and his father who wanted into the bathroom, again! And the son was looking directly at me. Eyes wide, mouth hanging open. I grinned at him, baring all my pearly whites and made a show of cramming Ben's face into my crotch more. Up and down, up and down.

The son didn't move. Didn't even say anything, or get up to summon the usher. I turned away, leaned my head back again, smiling. I knew he was still watching.

I could feel his eyes on us, trying to penetrate the dark, snatching glimpses of our naughty activity during the bright moments of the film.

Suddenly, Ben stopped and looked up at me, trying to catch his breath. "We need toys," he said.

"Toys?"

"Yeah, and lubricant, and mirrors, and a big bed. Preferably, one that rotates. I have all that at my apartment."

"You do?" I said, pleasantly surprised.

"Yup," he said, wiping at his mouth. "Let's blow this Popsicle stand and go to my place. Then we can get into some real action."

"You're happy that your theatre fantasy has been fulfilled," I asked, sceptically. I arched an eyebrow for emphasis. I kinda wanted to stay. He was in mid-fellatio after all. You can't just stop those sort of things half way, ya know!

He got up, eased out from my legs and sat in his seat again. "Buddy, we're just getting started."

I couldn't argue with that. So I managed to get myself into a more dignified position on the seat and pulled my pants back up. I could feel the slick wetness of his spit on my cock and thighs.

Then we collected ourselves and scooted out of there, arm in arm, big grins on our ass licking faces.

In the lobby, I heard a shout. Turning, I was expecting that damned manager again, banning me forever. Wouldn't have surprised me if the little pervert was up in the projection booth watching us and tugging one off.

But it was the son! He hurried over to me, getting real close. He pointedly ignore Ben.

He jammed a piece of paper in my hand, and said with an intense gaze, "Call me."

I glanced at the paper, the name Carl was written on it, with a phone number hastily scrawled across it. He dropped me a wink and turned and hurried away.

I watched the lovely wiggle of his tight rump as he walked away and mentally flagged it as a future tourist destination I just have to visit, and soon.

Ben was watching him, too. "Wonder if we should include him."

I smiled. Thank God he wasn't the jealous type. "No," I said. "That's for another future adventure." Then I took Ben by the arm again, walked over the pukey colored carpet and out into the sunshine.

We had an apartment to violate.

As for my little adventure with Ben I'll say this: Everyone should have a theatre going experience such as this one. And, as for the movie: Although I haven't a clue what it was called, or what it was about, it certainly was the best damn movie ever!

END

The Lustful Landscapers

<u>(Sausage Fest)</u>

Standing at the upstairs window of the master bedroom, Rick couldn't help but notice the landscaper outside, who had just arrived that morning for work.

Safely hidden behind partially closed curtains, he observed him circling the arrangements of flowers and plants, inspecting them. He was young, maybe nineteen or so, tall and in amazingly athletic shape.

Well, well, well, he thought. *Who* do we have here?

"Didn't you hear me?" Hank, his husband, said from the adjoining bathroom. He sounded quite annoyed. He always did.

Snapped back to reality he quickly turned away from the window. "Oh, sorry," he said, not really meaning it. "I was just watching the news." The television's screen was dark, so he quickly grabbed the remote from the bedside table and flicked it on. Best way to cover a lie was to at least make it believable.

"I asked if you were planning on doing anything useful with yourself, today," he said as he emerged from the bathroom. "As opposed to the big fat nothing you normally do." Hank's naked form was anything but impressive; balding head, pudgy belly covered in hair, pale skin making him look sallow and sick. His physique was a far cry from the toned one he had maintained way back when they were courting. Now Rick just found him repulsive. He turned back to the television, while trying not to make it look too obvious.

When he didn't answer immediately Hank glared at him. "Well? Where did you plan on spending more of my money? Maybe in the company of one of your other gold digging friends?"

Rick made an effort not to get angry. Fighting with Hank was useless as he could be completely unreasonable to the point of being childish. Instead, he looked him in the eyes and said, "Since it was your idea that I quit my job to begin with, and spend more time at home serving your needs, the least I could do is find some way I could enjoy myself."

Like with the landscaper, he thought to himself. He made an effort not to glance back outside. At least not while his husband was in the room.

Hank snorted, and went to the closet to get dressed. "Whatever," he said. "I'm beginning to not care what you do anymore as it only seems to revolve around draining my bank account." He glowered at Rick. "You certainly aren't draining anything else."

Rick shivered. Going down on his husband was the furthest thing from pleasurable in his mind. He had lost that privilege years ago.

But Rick knew that his spending habits were not the real issue, here. Last night he refused to make love to Hank, as he had done each night now for several weeks. Hank's lack of respect for him, coupled with his ugly physique, made him less desirous than ever before.

Rick made a point of shooting a look directly at his shrivelled penis, and said, "I'm beginning to find that your money is the only thing worth spending time on." He immediately regretted snapping at him but felt he had to defend himself, at least a little.

Hank scowled, but said nothing. He turned to the closet and busied himself with finishing getting dressed. Their pointless fighting had grown more frequent over the years. Neither one getting the upper hand on the other. It was starting to wear them both down.

There could only be one inevitable outcome to this slow spiral they found themselves in. Perhaps, since things could not be salvaged, and coupled with the fact that neither really wanted to do anything to heal the damage, he should think about doing things only for himself now.

For his own pleasure, specifically.

Rick found himself stealing a glimpse outside the window, again. The landscaper was squatting down next to the edge of a bed of red roses, moving some large rocks, tanned arm muscles flexing. Rick's eyes widened. From this position he was able to see up his shorts. One hairless testicle had slipped free of its confines to dangled downward; revealing itself only to Rick. The fact the landscaper hadn't noticed made it feel all the more exciting.

Rick unconsciously licked his lips. *Oh my*.

Rick quickly looked away as he noticed, from the corner of his eye, that Hank had finished dressing, and had walked over to where his jacket hung from the back of the bedroom's only bench.

They use to make love in that bench, he thought sullenly. Mad and passionate love. But that seemed only a muted memory, one experienced by someone else. He couldn't even bare to think of such a thing with his husband now. They had become more like roommates, than a lovers. And temperamental roommates at that.

Slipping on his suit jacket Hank said, "I don't know what I've done to you to turn you into such a limp dick. But I'm starting to get tired of it."

He had done it entirely to himself, Rick thought. Hank treated him poorly, and even went out of his way to ignore him. His belittling comments had now become a part of their every day conversation. Still, Rick had heard all of this before and found that now, more than ever, he had stopped caring at what those words might mean.

"You are not the only one who's getting tired of the way things are," he said. "Maybe our lives need to be spiced up a little. Without the other souring the mood."

Suddenly, he envisioned himself looking up at the landscaper, that dangling testicle fully in his suckling mouth. He shuddered with pleasure.

Hank frowned at him, and pulled on his jacket. His face had turned red. "Spice things up a little? What the hell does that mean?"

Rick tried to make an effort to only stare at the TV. He didn't respond. Let Hank sweat a little.

"Fine," Hank said, when he didn't explain himself. He grabbed his keys and his cell phone from the top of the dresser (they had made love on that, too) and headed for the bedroom door. Before leaving, he stopped and looked at him. "You know what? I don't care. Do what you want. I think I'm going to stay late at work tonight. We have a new assistant now and he's very cute."

Rick was surprised to find himself getting angry at this. He glared at Hank but said nothing. No need to stoke the fires further.

Hank grinned at his reaction. "That's right," he said. "Hot, and well muscled in all the right places. And I can guarantee he would appreciate me a lot more than you have." Convinced he had scored an emotional punch Hank turned away and left.

Rick suppressed the urge to run after him. He wanted to scream, throw things at him, shattering glass. But he didn't. Making a tremendous effort to control himself, staring at the TV, not hearing what the newscasters were chattering on about. Only when he heard Hank slammed the car door and drive away did he find he had been holding his breath.

Rick gasped. What a bastard. Why had he bothered to marry someone like that? Maybe there was something to what he had said. Hank's money had become the only thing about him he was interested in now. But it certainly didn't start that way. They had been drifting apart for years, despite his best efforts to counter the erosion of their relationship.

Not once had he been unfaithful to Hank. Although, there had been many temptations and opportunities. He was sexy after all. He had been told so, on many occasions, and not by his husband.

And now Hank practically threatened him with infidelity? Well, then, he thought. If he started it, maybe I should take him up on that offer.

Rick stood at the window, again. The landscaper was unravelling a hose, only half paying attention to what he was doing. He was wearing sunglasses, which gave him an almost rock star look. His mind was obviously elsewhere. Was he thinking of his girlfriend, perhaps? Boyfriend? Strangely, Rick felt a twinge of jealousy at the thought.

Rick was wearing his robe, and it was partially open. Without thinking of it, his hand had drifted down the exposed part of his body. His fingers grasped his penis. It was getting hard. Very hard.

Well, he thought. That definitely wasn't because of his husband.

He started jerking himself, slowly, allowing his fingers to rub over his prick. Using his other hand, he grabbed one of his pectorals, squeezing it and pinching its nipple.

He opened his eyes, and gasped. Down below the landscaper was looking up at him, the coil of hose now forgotten. Despite the fact the sunglasses masked his eyes, he knew he had been watching him.

And still *was* watching him.

Suddenly, realizing he had just been caught, the landscaper looked away, and quickly turned and disappeared into the garden's supply shed.

Rick found himself intensely aroused by the young man's reaction. Still, he had enough composure to close his robe and tie it up. His erection pressed against the fabric, demanding to be released.

If Hank wanted him to do something useful with his day, then he would do exactly that!

Feeling giddy, Rick put on his slippers and went downstairs. Their house was quite literally a mansion. Many rooms packed with things they never really used. It really was just empty of any life, too large for just two people.

The house was a perfect analogy for their marriage. Empty and pointless.

He padded into the kitchen, and opened the refrigerator. It was packed full of food, most of which would go to waste. He found what he was looking for, a bottle of champagne. He then grabbed a pair of wine glasses, which clinked as he walked, and he went outside, through the sliding glass door in the adjoining dining room.

The air was hot on his skin, and he suspected that not all the heat he felt wasn't all because of the sun.

The landscaper had not yet emerged from the shed, no doubt mortified he could be in trouble.

Poor thing, he thought. I better do something to fix that right away.

As he approached the shed's door, the landscaper suddenly emerged. He looked surprised to see him, and maybe a little flush.

"Oh, hello," Rick said with the biggest smile he could manage. Since Hank had paid for his teeth to be so pearly white he may as well put them to good use.

"Hi," the landscaper said, a little sheepishly. Was he shy, or just a little startled to find the masturbating hunk suddenly outside in front of him?

It was then that Rick noticed the sagging bulge in the front of the landscaper's shorts.

Well now, Rick thought. What could explain that? Had he been masturbating, *too*? Maybe they had something in common.

He was secretly thrilled at the prospect the landscaper had been satisfying himself in the privacy of the shack. Because of Rick.

"I saw you working, and thought I'd come out and see how things were going. You're new, aren't you?"

The landscaper managed a small smile, and said, "Uh, yeah," he stammered. He towered over Rick, who pegged him at six foot two at least. Much taller than Hank, who was about the same height as Rick. He had always found taller men very appealing. Now he could see why.

The landscaper continued, "Yeah, I'm new. Your husband just hired me. I know what I'm suppose to do. I've done this before." He smiled and Rick's day got just a little brighter.

Rick smiled at this. He did hope the landscaper knew what he was doing. Although, the prospect of him being inexperienced also had an allure. What Rick really wanted to do was find out first hand which it was!

"I'm Rick."

"I'm Steve."

Mmmm. Steve.

"I brought us something to drink," he said. "I hope you're thirsty." Rick's eyes dropped to the bulge in Steve's shorts. It hadn't changed, but it hadn't gone away, either.

Whether Steve noticed or not, Rick couldn't tell. Steve said, "No. That's okay. I wouldn't want to bother you." His voice was deep, even commanding, although he seemed to lack the confidence that comes with age.

"That's alright," Rick said and held out the champagne bottle. Steve hesitated, either with the fact he was about to have a drink with his employer's life partner, or that fact that Rick was actually offering him alcohol first thing in the morning.

Rick wiggled it at him encouragingly. He took it. He frowned boyishly at the cap and its metal cage work.

"Just twist it," Rick offered. I'll give you something else to twist, he thought.

Steve did so, and Rick watched the muscles in his arms move with the effort. He was *very* athletic, Rick decided. Once the cap had been worked out as far as it would go, he braced the bottom of the bottle against his stomach. The movement pulled up the front of his shirt, and his abs showed prominently.

Rick found himself drooling.

With the bottle braced, and abs at the ready, he used both thumbs to push at the cork. It slowly started to give way.

Rick then said, "I saw you watching me as I played with my cock."

Steve gasped, and the cap suddenly launched with a loud pop! Bubbly froth shot out of the bottle in an arch, and Steve held it away from himself.

Rick felt a sudden impulse, and acted on it. As the frothy arch subsided, he quickly stepped forward, grabbed the neck of the bottle and stuck the end of it in his mouth.

He gulped loudly, as the bubbles hit against the back of his throat. He looked up at Steve as he drank. Steve's face was locked onto his, his mouth open in obvious shock.

When Rick couldn't handle any more, he pulled the bottle out, somehow coughing and laughing at the same time. Much of the champagne had dribbled on his robe and he wiped at it coyly. "Oh look what I've done," he said. "Can't walk around all wet now, can I?" And with that he slowly untied his robe and let it fall to the ground. The sun felt wonderful on his skin but not nearly as good as how Steve's eyes felt.

Rick stood before him for a few moments posing seductively. He felt incredibly sexy, like a Greek god.

Steve stood dumbfounded still gripping the bottle with both hands. This was not what he expected when he woke up for work this morning. Not wanting him to run away Rick stepped lightly forward and cupped his hands, which were gripping the bottle, and slowly began to lick champagne from its neck. As he worked at he made sure to look at Steve alluringly.

"Whoa," Steve said.

Rick paused with the licking and sucked at the lip of the bottle looking at Steve with a questioning arched brow. "Whoa, as in you want me to stop?"

When Steve didn't respond right away Rick noticed a movement, and his eyes dropped down. Steve was fumbling a hand in his shorts, but his erection had caught on the fabric and he couldn't get out.

Careful not to laugh at him, Rick smiled and placed a restraining hand on the front of the shorts while he took the bottle, and gently placed it on the ground. Then he took Steve's free hand and guided him back a few steps so he could kneel on the robe and not have his knees on the concrete. Thanks to many years of practice Rick knew how to get an excited man's pants off without causing any damage. When they were all the way off Steve stepped out of them by placing his hand on Rick's head for balance. This manly touch excited Rick, and he cast the shorts aside.

Steve was fully erect, with only a small pronouncement of hair above it. The rest of the skin on his groin was amazingly hairless. Rick approved of his grooming, and showed him.

Unable to contain himself further Rick gripped the base of the shaft leaned forward and put Steve's swollen prick in his mouth. He swirled his tongue around around him enjoying the taste of his hot flesh. He made sure that he got as much of his dick in his mouth. Then he sucked. With his free hand he massaged Steve's hairless balls.

While Rick slowly worked, he looked up at him. Steve's head was tilted back and his mouth was open slightly with obvious pleasure. One of his hands was still on the back of Rick's head, almost as if to ensure he didn't get away, and Rick found that particularly arousing. Slowly stroking him Rick followed his hand up and down with his mouth, sucking with determination. Rick found Steve really liked it when he partially gagged on his swollen cock.

Rick did this for several long moments, both of them enjoying it immensely. Rick didn't want him to cum, not yet. There were things still to be done with this young buck.

With one final suck, Rick kept stroking his shaft, and said, "Let's move to the bench. I want to ride you for a while." Steve nodded in agreement. Rick stood, and while guiding Steve by his dick, gently pulled him over to one of the long granite bench nearby, in a small clearing in the vast garden.

Rick made Steve sit facing towards him. He placed a hand on either side of his face and said, "I have something that really needs tending to." Then he stepped forward a little and presented Steve's face with his cock.

Steve kissed it hungrily, licking and at sucking the length of him. Rick held him there for a very long time, enjoying the feeling as he played with his swollen member. What Steve lacked in experience he more than made up for with enthusiasm. Steve grabbed Rick's ass with both hands and squeezed. Occasionally Rick would thrust deeper into Steve's mouth, and Rick enjoyed hearing, and feeling, him moan.

With the warm sun on his back, and the young stud now sucking eagerly at him, Rick knew this was the best decision he ever made.

After a time Rick pulled himself out of Steve's hungry mouth, bent down and kissed his lips. He said, "Time for my morning exercise." And with that Rick turned around and straddled him. Squatting down, he took Steve's dick and guided to his ass-hole, then inside himself, until Rick had slid down its full-length. Putting his hands on Steve's muscular thighs, just above the knees for balance, he started to move up and down. Steve grabbed at his ass while leaning backwards, helping him with the movements.

Rick rode him, moving slowly at first until he found a wonderful rhythm. Then he started to go faster, always making sure he slid up Steve's entire length, almost until it seemed he would escape his ass-hole's grip, only to suddenly slam down and smack loudly against the flesh of his legs. Many minutes past like this. Riding him on and on.

After a while Rick switch the position around, so they were facing each other. Rick smiled at him, as Steve did to him. But Steve's focus quickly switched to Ricks pectorals. As Rick slammed up and down, he sucked and teethed at his nipples

nipples. All the while, Steve jerked Rick off as he moved up and down.

Soon their breathing was in sync, and Rick started to grind against him, mostly to give his aching legs a break from their hard effort. Rick pushed him back against the bench, hands on his muscular chest, and vigorously wiggled his ass back and forth. Steve groaned, and then gritted his teeth. Rick could hear the their flesh made smacking against each other; sliding along each other.

Rick smiled. He was surprised Steve had lasted as long as he did. Not losing his rhythm, Rick leaned forward and grabbed Steve's head. In his ear Rick whispered with hot breath, "Cum inside me, little boy. I want you to cum all inside me. Blow my head of with your load."

Steve moaned, and held Rick's hips firmly, helping him grind harder now that he was allowed to finally climax. Rick watched his handsome face, with joyous anticipation.

As if to aid him, Rick dug his nails into Steve's firm pectorals, and sucked on one of his earlobes. Moments passed, sucking, grinding, pleasurable raking of nails.

And Steve popped. With a tremendous moan, he bucked beneath Rick. Rick laughed, swinging one hand in the air above his head, and yelled, "Yeehaa!" like a regular rodeo rider.

Over and over Steve writhed, until he had spent his entire load inside of him. And Rick drank in every moment of Steve's pleasure.

Rick fell forward, and they embraced each other, both covered in sweat, exhausted from the intensity of their passion.

They held each other for a while until Rick said, "That was the best landscaping work I've had in a while."

Steve laughed.

"No," Rick said. "I'm serious. You helped reshape my, uh, fertile landscape quite well."

"Well, I am glad I could be of service to you, sir."

Rick made a show of pouting, "Don't call me that!"

"What?"

"Sir! It makes me sound old."

Steve arched an inquisitive brow. "Well, how old are you?"

Only a young man could get away with asking such a question and not get killed.

Rick thought about it a moment, but decided to be honest with him. "I'm thirty-one."

Steve's eyebrows shot up, and his mouth hung open. "Whoa! No way!" And laughed.

Rick started to feel a little self conscience. "Why," he asked after a moments hesitation. "How old are you?"

Steve regained his composure, and, as if for emphasis, removed his sunglasses for the first time. Piercing blue eyes regarded him wryly. "I'm nineteen, *Sir*." He grinned.

Rick was shocked. "Oh, my God!" he practically shouted. "I've robbed the cradle!"

"Yeah," Steve agreed. "But in the best way possible."

They both laughed at this, and he fell into his muscular arms, again.

From behind where they were sitting a young man's voice said sternly, "What the hot staggering fuck is going on here, Steve?"

They both jolted up and looked. A handsome blonde guy, no older than nineteen, stood a short distance away from them. He was very slim, but wonderfully defined. His muscles strained at the confining fabric of his t-shirt. In one hand he held a paper bag which had a fast food emblem on the side of it. His other hand was firmly placed on his hip.

The new guy looked pissed.

"Eddie!" blurted Steve. "It's not what you think." And with that stupid comment, he firmly pushed Rick up off him, or to be more exact, eased himself *out* of Rick. Both of them stood up.

Eddie was furious. "Not what it looks like? You idiot, you're both naked! Together! And your dick was inside him!"

"No, I... I" Steve stammered. He was out of his element, and knew he was caught red handed. Or at least with his hand in the cookie jar, as it were.

Eddie continued to rage, "You ass-hole! Is this how you treat me? By fucking other people?" He turned to go.

Rick was stunned when Steve unexpectedly said: "Babe, I was just warming him up for you."

The other two looked equally shocked at Steve's gall. What balls it took to say something like that.

But Steve continued before Eddie could recover. "You know how we've talked about getting into a three-way. In fact you mentioned it last week."

Eddie held up his hand. "Wait, you're trying to make me believe you planned on this?" He involuntarily glanced at Rick's naked body, giving it a quick once over with his eyes. He looked away, and Rick found himself secretly thrilled at the look.

Eddie shook his head. "I ain't buying it."

Steve said, "Hey, I knew you were coming today to bring me lunch." He pointed at the fast food bag in his hand. "But this thing with, uh... what was you're name again?"

Rick laughed, despite himself. "Rick."

"Yeah, Rick. It just suddenly happened."

Rick shrugged, "I jumped him. He didn't have much of a chance. I mean," he stretched his arms up and gave a sexy pose, "could you really blame the poor guy?"

Eddie's brow furrowed, but his eyes betrayed him by raking Rick's body again, but with far more interest. "I don't know..." he said.

Rick smiled and walked over to the young man. Eddie didn't back away, nor did he flinch when Rick put his hands gently on his shoulders. "I'd like to jump you, too." Rick offered a big grin. "He is worth sharing, isn't he?"

They both looked over at Steve, how was obviously very happy with the way the confrontation had done an about face. His dick was getting hard again, as he watched them.

Eddie suddenly smiled for the first time. Rick quickly took advantage of this, before the opportunity was lost, and kissed him. At first Eddie was resistant, but slowly yielded to the probing tongue that flickered at his lips. He opened his mouth more fully, and Rick sought his tongue with his own.

They kissed like this for a while, hungrily delving into the other. Rick was pleasantly surprised when Eddie dropped the bag of fast food, and gripped Rick's nipples, squeezing them. One hand eventually went down Rick's stomach, and latched onto his hard cock.

Rick embraced him closer, with his own hands sliding down the other man's back, down inside the back of his shorts, and he grabbed Eddie's firm butt cheeks. They both chuckled.

Several moments passed like this, and Rick felt that Eddie was getting more and more impassioned with each passing moment.

Eddie pulled away, with a final suck at Rick's lips and asked, "He came inside you, didn't he?" It wasn't an accusation, nor angry in anyway, so Rick felt safe in nodding in the affirmative.

He glanced over at Steve, who was busy stroking his dick, but he kept his distance wanting to just enjoy the show, for now.

"Then, let me have some of it," he said, and Rick's eyes widened at the implications.

Eddie dropped to knees, turned Rick around, and forced his face up between Rick's ass cheeks. Eddie licked at Rick's butt hole experimentally, ensuring he got to taste every small part of it; rimming it all around, licking Rick's taint, with his nose pressed into Rick's firm flesh. Lips firmly affixed Eddie sucked in between his lips and teethed his anus gently with his tongue.

Rick moaned and reached around to run his fingers through the soft blonde hair, pressing the younger man's head against him while he sucked his ass hungrily. Eddie worked his tongue deep up inside him, slurping all the while. Eventually, he was able to suck some of Steve's cum out of its warm and wet home.

After a few moments of concentrated effort, and with his mouth full, Eddie stood, and they both grinned at each other. Then Rick crouched a little, so Eddie could lean over him, and with careful aim, allowed the cum to dribble out of his mouth, down his chin and into Rick's open mouth. When everything had sloppily been spit out, Rick stood, and the two men kissed; Steve's seed was exchanged noisily back and forth.

When both men were done, they both swallowed loudly. They then kissed and licked at each others faces, getting all the sticky drops that were missed.

Steve was stroking faster, and Rick walked over to him, while leading Eddie by the hand. "Not so fast," Rick said.

Rick looked to Eddie, "Do you want more?"

Eddie nodded eagerly, "Oh, I'm still very, very hungry."

Rick laid Eddie down on the bench with his legs spread wide, ass exposed far all to appreciate. Rick then bent over, one knee on the lower part of the bench, his face bare inches from Eddie's tasty ass-hole. He looked over his shoulder at Steve and said, "Fuck my ass, landscaper. I'm your boss, and I'm giving you an order." He wiggle his butt invitingly at him.

Steve nodded, and smacked Rick's butt hard and loud. Rick bit his lip with the pleasant pain, and then turned to Eddie's ass-hole. He started to lick it, but also took turns sucking the young man's ball sack, too. Noisily, he would lick and slurp one, and then the other. Eddie jerked off with vigour.

Eventually, Eddie's ass-hole and balls glistened with Rick's spit.

Steve bent over and spit as well, right on Rick's awaiting ass-hole, lubing it up for his throbbing cock. He gently rubbed his prick against it, then, very slowly eased it inside him. Rick gasped, but continued to suck noisily at Eddie's beautiful butt.

Soon Steve was all the way inside Rick's ass, and he began to pump against him. Rick's butt cheeks jiggled enticingly, and Steve smacked them repeatedly.

This went on for several long minutes, and then they switched positions, Eddie bent over for Steve, while licking at Rick's raw ass-hole, and sucked at his balls. Long wonderful minutes passed as they pleasured one another. The hot sun barely matching the intensity of the heat they generated with each other.

The sounds of laughter, pleasure, slurping and smacking echoed through the thick foliage of the garden.

Eventually, Steve came again. He withdrew from Rick's hole, and came all over his ass cheeks. He squeezed his cock, making sure every little bit ended up on him. Eddie sat up, gave Steve's prick a sloppy kiss, and then started to lick Rick's glistening butt. Over and over he did this, getting every last little bit of Steve's spent seed.

Eddie smacked Rick's ass, and then as the other two watched expectantly, Eddie swallowed.

"Tastes much better the second time around," Eddie said. They all laughed.

They then lay together on the bench. Steve in the middle, the other two men under each arm, and practically on top of him, as there was hardly any room.

They stroked each others throbbing dicks, and dozed in the sun.

Rick was elated, but also more than a little disappointed. This wouldn't be happening again, as there was more than his pleasure he was ensuring with this little tryst.

What Rick didn't tell them was that the whole perimeter of the house was covered by close circuit security cameras. Every naughty thing they had done had been fully recorded for review later.

And Rick couldn't wait to show that ungrateful husband of his, exactly how he could be properly appreciated!

END.

The Pizza Guy is Packing

(His Big Fat Sausage)

"I've had it with cheating men!" cried Ryan into his cell phone.

His friend, Paul, who was on the receiving end of this declaration, tried to calm him down. "Oh, Ryan, honey," he said. "They're not all bad. Some of them are genuinely cowed enough to know they shouldn't mess with man-bitches like us."

Neither man felt such a statement was close to the truth, but it certainly helped Ryan a little to think it was. At least for the moment. Was he ready to give up on men all together?

Ryan paced his apartment living room. "I don't care to find out anymore. So many games, so many lies. A guy can't get anything honest from someone who can't manage where his penis goes. They just can't be trusted."

He had reason to be angry. Carl, his boyfriend... ex-boyfriend... had just admitted to him, not fifteen minutes ago, that he had been unfaithful to him for the last two months of their relationship. With some waiter at a bar he frequented.

The coward had told him over the phone, too. He didn't have the nerve, or the balls, to tell him to his face. He would have liked to have punched him! Or at least scratched his eyes out.

Paul continued to try and calm his friend down. "Yeah, they're scum. They can't be trusted. Maybe you should just, I dunno, maybe take a break from serious relationships for a little bit. I know this just happened and all, but maybe this was for the best."

Ryan had paced into the bedroom and caught his reflection in the closet mirror. He was still in a bathrobe, having showered in preparation for going out with Carl that evening. He gave his body an appraising once over. He was hot dammit! Why would any man in his right mind even entertain the idea of screwing around behind his back? Especially *this* lovely back! He turned and lifted up the robe exposing a very firm, and pleasantly shaped, muscular ass.

No more of this honey-dew for him!

"I know, I know," Ryan said. "It just hurts. I thought we had something truly meaningful. But I guess it wasn't meaningful enough." He gave his own ass a smack and was pleased that it barely shook. "Maybe I should just pick up some random piece of meat at the bar and screw the hell out of it."

"Yes!" Paul shouted. "Nothing better than cheap meaningless sex with a stranger to help you get through times of trouble."

Just then the downstairs buzzer rang.

"Who's that?" asked Paul.

"Oh, shoot. I forgot I ordered a pizza." Carl had called him right after he had placed it. He buzzed in whoever it was without answering.

"Wait a second, sister," said Paul, conspiratorially. "What if he's a hunk?"

Ryan scoffed. "No, it's always this little fat guy who smells of sweat and cheese."

"You should *do* him!"

"No way!" Ryan shuddered. Just the thought of it made his skin crawl.

"Or, it could be someone different. A moonlighting underwear model."

Ryan's brow furrowed. "Wow, you have quite the imagination. Well, if that were the case, he'd get one hell of a tip outta me, tonight."

"That a girl!" cried Paul.

Ryan was only half joking. It would take a lot to get him to indulge in a casual quickie with a stranger.

There was a knock at the door. Ryan took a moment to look himself over in the living room mirror. The robe hung half open, so he synched it closed. It accentuated broad shoulders. His muscular legs were bare for all to see. The robe only just covered his ass. He hadn't put on any underwear after he finished showering, and there certainly wasn't any time now to put some on.

I do look damn sexy, though, he thought to himself. At least mister chubby from the pizza place will get a little bit of an eye full.

While he walked to the door, Paul was chanting in the phone, "Hot sex! Hot sex! Hot sex!"

Ryan could only roll his eyes. As if.

He peered through the peek hole.

A tall dashing hunk of a man was standing out there. Holding a pizza box. His pizza box.

"Uh," was all Ryan was able to say.

Paul immediately pounced. "What? WHAT?!"

Ryan found himself whispering, his eye glued to the hole, drinking in the beefcake outside. "It's not the usual guy. He's..." *Gorgeous.*

"So? Is he handsome, or just handsome enough?" asked Paul, intrigued with his friend's change of tone. "Either will do for now."

Ryan realized he had been staring at him entirely too long. He took a deep breath and opened the door.

The peephole view did not do this walking Greek God justice. Tall, chiseled features, and perfectly muscled, he gave Ryan a pearly white smile.

"Hi," he said. "Did you order a pizza?"

Ryan was momentarily speechless. He was also alarmed to feel his cock start to take notice and perk up from between his thighs.

"Yeah," he managed to stammer smiling, still a little shocked. He stepped back, letting him inside. He closed the door behind him.

He had forgotten his cell phone was in his free hand, until he dimly heard Paul cry out: "Do him! Screw his brains out! Give him a tip he'll never forget!"

Ryan quickly hung up. The pizza boy... man... stud, crooked a questioning eyebrow. He managed not to blush. "My friend wants pizza, too," he finally said, and immediately felt ridiculous.

He continued smiling politely, "Our pizza has that effect on folks." His eyes were an incredible piercing blue, and they glanced down at his robe, and then at his legs before quickly returning to his eyes again.

He was surprised to find himself thrilled at this.

"You're not the usual delivery boy."

"Oh, you probably get Andrew," his voice was deep, confident. The kind you wouldn't mind having whispering instructions in your ear. "He called in sick so I had to pick up the slack."

Ryan nodded, dully. This guy was a lot to take in. He suddenly found himself wondering just how much that would be, and in how many positions. "I've never seen you before. Are you new there?"

"New? Oh, more than that. I'm the owner."

He looked down at the company name on the pizza box. It said Mike's Pizza Palace. "You're Mike?" he said, incredulous.

"The big boss man himself," he said with a confident grin.

Ryan found he was most definitely hungry, now. And no longer just for pizza.

He was struck with a strong impulse and felt an overwhelming urge to act on it. Paul was right. Meaningless sex with a stranger could be exactly what he needs right now. Especially with this particular handsome stranger.

"Oh, uh, please bring it in the living room," he said, walking away from him. He more or less had to follow. As he turned he sneaked a look at his wedding finger. No ring..

Good.

Ryan also noted his eyes fell on his butt as he talked to him over his shoulder.

"Right over there, please," he pointed at the big coffee table which was between the couch and the easy chair.

Mike gave a short nod to him as he passed. He inhaled his wake as he did so, and liked the hint of his cologne, and the slight tinge of sweat. Most likely from working hard most of the night.

He yearned to make him sweat some more.

He placed the box on the table, and as he turned toward him, he quickly undid his robes, and let them fall to the floor. He put his hands on his hips and bent a knee slighting for enticing emphasis. His bare cock, now almost erect, was free to salute the room.

Mike froze, eyes locked on his naked form. Ryan was sexy as all hell, and he could see Mike thought the same.

"Well, Mike of the Pizza Palace," he said, with fire in his eyes, and a seductive

tone in his voice. "I have a way I can pay you properly for that pizza."

Mike's jaw dropped, and his eyes roved over him. He was appropriately shell shocked, and took several moments to compose himself.

Who could blame him?

"I, uh…" he stammered.

Deciding to take his initiative even further Ryan didn't want Mike to have to decide on his own. He walked forward, engorged dick wiggling hypnotically, and grabbed at Mike's t-shirt. He only flinched just slightly, as if his brain was only now catching up with unfolding events, but he smiled and yielded.

He chuckled and raised his arms so he could pull the it off of him.

His chest did not disappoint. Ridged muscles lined his body and stomach. His pectorals were the size of dinner plates and his arms were hard as tempered steel, and almost as thick as tree trunks.

Ryan ran his hands over his barrelled chest. "You lift a lot of heavy pizzas to get a body like that?" he asked teasingly.

"Something like that," he said. His hands rubbed Ryan's shoulders, and up and down his arms. Then he cupped his pectorals, rubbing them. Ryan found his hands were calloused and strong, just the way he liked them.

He grabbed at Mike's belt and undid it with a playful grunt. Mike smiled and let him work at it. When unbuckled, he unzipped Mike's fly, then squatted down in front of him, pulling his pants down. He managed to work them to his hips, and with one final tug, yanked them down to his knees.

It was then that a huge dick popped out of them, partially engorged. The sudden motion of the pants had freed this large piece of meat from its lair, and it swung out and hit Ryan on the side of the nose.

"Oh, my God!" Ryan gasped. Mike smiled down at him. He blinked in astonishment. "I don't remember ordering this!" He giggled, amazed.

"It's a side special. For hot, sexy customers only," Mike said.

He pulled off Mike's shoes, and then aided him in removing his pants from his ankles. He then turned his attention to the now large erect penis in front of him, demanding attention.

Grabbing it eagerly, Ryan stroking it up and down, marvelling at its thickness, and heft. Stealing his courage, he then put it in his mouth, and started to suck. It was large, but he had managed this size before.

Mike sighed with the sudden feel of his warm wet mouth on his prick, and the feel of his lips moving up and down his shaft. Because of his size, the sound of Ryan's slurping and occasional gagging was more prominent.

Up and down he worked him. Long minutes of concentrated effort, with his mouth made his dick glisten with spit, creating a slight foam at its base. Some spit eventually dribbled down to his balls to dangle there in an elastic string.

Satisfied he had properly welcomed him into his home, he leaned back a bit for a breather, and gasped.

Ryan motioned to the easy chair, "Sit down. I have an idea."

"I like your ideas so far," Mike said with wide appreciative eyes. He did as he was told.

Ryan flipped open the pizza box, exposing the steaming contents. As he tried to pick at a ring of green pepper he squealed from its heat. Finding one that suited his needs, Ryan turned towards him, and Mike's eyes widened at what he had in mind.

Gingerly, he broke it at one point, then wrapped the green pepper around the base of his thick cock. Because he was so well shaved, it rested against his skin and he hissed slightly, but not with great pain.

"You okay?" Ryan asked coyly.

"Oh, yeah," Mike said through gritted teeth. "I knew my pizza's were hot but not *this* hot."

Ryan grinned up at him, then swirled his tongue around his prick. He took his dick in his mouth, and slowly worked his way down its length, occasionally pausing to wiggle his head back and forth to help it past the hook at the back of his throat. Mike gasped, as his tongue poked out of the bottom of his gaping mouth. His girth had forced his mouth wide, stretching his lips around him. Spittle gathered in sticky strands at the corners.

With amazing patience, Ryan neither gagged, or pulled back. He gazed up at Mike with big eyes, and his tongue prodded the green pepper until he managed to catch it. Then, very slowly, he slid back up Mike's length, green pepper in tow.

Sucking him at the tip, the green pepper dangled from his mouth. Then he leaned back, plucking it in his fingers and smiling at him triumphantly.

"Impressive!" Mike said, laughing. "My turn to do a trick."

He eased Ryan up off his knees, and had him sit in the easy chair, this time. Ryan spread his legs by hooking his knees over the chair arms, exposing his very well shaved balls, and *very* hard cock to him. Ryan rubbed at his ball-sack playfully.

"Do as you please, pizza man," Ryan said while teething the tip of one of his fingers.

"Oh, I will," Mike returned. With one finger he dipped into the tomato sauce of the pizza. Careful to get enough, he then slowly spread it around testicles, smearing them completely with sauce.

It was Ryan's turn to grit his teeth from the heat, as Mike worked his grip up and down his dick. Then Mike leaned forward, and with strong hands firmly holding his legs wide at the thighs, he started to lick.

Up and down, then all around, he licked and slurped. When a little sauce dripped down into the slight hollow at Ryan's ass-hole, he slurped it up. He then stayed there, rimming his ass-hole with his tongue.

Ryan gasped with pleasure, massaging his pecs, pinching at their erect nipples.

Then Mike returned his attention to Ryan's cock, taking long deliberate licks, making sure he wasn't finished until it was completely cleaned of tomato sauce.

Mike grinned up at him and said, "My special sauce never tasted so damn good."

Ryan smiled back and said, "Glad to finally be on your menu."

Mike then stood, cock hard and ready. He leaned forward, so he was hovering over Ryan, and bent his dick as far as it would go. He stuck his prick into Ryan's waiting ass-hole, smearing tomato sauce everywhere. Ryan gasped, and grabbed onto Mike's hips. Mike paused, and said, "Can I make a quick delivery, sir?"

"Please do!" Ryan said.

And with that, Mike suddenly slammed the entire length of his long dick deep inside him. Ryan gasped with the hard penetration. Mike then lifted his butt up again, so his entire length was nearly unsheathed from him, and slammed it down again.

Over and over he did this, getting faster and faster. Ryan moaned with each pelvic thrust. Long wonderful minutes passed as Mike slammed Ryan's ass again and again. Eventually, the intensity got to be so much Ryan's eyes rolled upwards showing only their whites.

Mike reached around Ryan's neck and pulled against his head slightly, so as to cut off some of the circulation. He gasped for air while Mike continued his relentless hammering. He eased off his head only when Ryan seemed close to passing out.

Then he slowed, making easy gyrating motions with his hips. He wanted to give Ryan a little time to recover before giving him what was about to happen next.

When Ryan seemed okay, Mike slipped out of him and Ryan's ass gave a wet fart. Mike then turned him around and pushed him on the chair so his upper body leaning against the back of it. His beautiful sweaty torso hung over the back edge.

Mike perched behind him, and smacked his incredible ass. It shook only slightly, being so firm.

Then he eased his dick into Ryan's ass-hole again, which was now sweaty and covered in tomato sauce. Making sure Ryan was firmly pressed up against the chair, hands holding his hips tightly, Mike began to pump back and forth. Each time he slammed Ryan's ass he grunted with the force of it. Mike could feel the bottom of his cock rub hard against the inside of Ryan and he knew Ryan felt it, too.

Again, he was relentless in his pounding. Over and over. Ryan gasped and moaned and dug his fingers into the chair. He was almost certain Mike was going to pound him straight through it.

The apartment filled with the ceaseless smacking of flesh on flesh. Punctuated with their mutual moans of pleasure.

Eventually, Mike grabbed Ryan's arms, and pulled them back by the elbows, forcing him to arch his back. His shaggy blonde hair dangled down to almost brush against his shoulders, and shook with each hard thrust. Mike began to slam against him even harder and he moaned more deeply.

On the other side of the living room was a mirror. In the reflection, Mike could see Ryan's firm muscles vibrating with the harsh pounding rhythm. His mouth was open, eyes were closed, and his brow was furrowed with gritting pleasure.

Over and over; again and again Mike tapped that ass, until he could see that Ryan was getting red where their flesh smacked against one an other.

Mike could not keep up this relentless pace. With both the feeling of him rubbing wetly inside him, and seeing Ryan's wonderfully firm flesh vibrating with his effort, he found himself about to explode.

"I'm gonna cum!" he practically shouted.

Quickly, Ryan pulled his body forward so as to unsheathe Mike's enormous dick from him, and he spun around. Mike then stood, stroking his cock vigorously. Ryan placed the bottom of his open mouth against the base of his prick. His tongue tickled at it eagerly, and his eyes stared up at him with hunger.

Mike stroked faster, and soon exploded with a loud moan. He semen spat out all over Ryan; many hot squirts into his mouth which slid down his tongue and pooled at the back of his throat. Over his face in long sticky strands that splayed across his cheeks and forehead. In the corner of one eye, down his chin, and some even got into his blonde hair.

As Mike sagged with completion, Ryan made a dramatic show of swallowing.

He smacked his mouth, and rolled his tongue around his lips, getting every white bit. A long thick strand still hung from his chin as he grinned widely up at him.

Ryan then grabbed Mike's dick again, and sucked it as his erection faded, nursing the last of his load. He wanted every little bit of that special sauce.

It was while he was doing this, and looking up at the exhausted pleasure in Mike's face, that he made a wondrous conclusion:

He needed to order out for pizza more often, dammit!

END

Getting Neighbourly

(Sausage Fest)

That morning, Peter woke to find himself in one of his moods: hot, bothered, and craving for a little trouble.

"Today, I think I'm gonna get me some," he declared with triumph.

Intent on doing something about it, he called in sick to work. As the assistant editor for a celebrity gossip web site, he knew skipping out for even a day would cost him later on. But, today, he just wanted to experience some of the things he had written about first hand. Why should famous people be the only ones allowed to have all the kinky fun?

Having never played hooky before, he found making an impulsive decision like this exhilarating.

His cell warbled, and his heart leaped into his throat. Was work checking on his fib *already*?

He picked it up and looked at the call display. He laughed. No, it was Tim, his best friend in the whole world. Peter knew Tim had quite the adventurous side. Maybe he should find out just how adventurous it could be?

"Hey, Tim! Why the early morning call?" he said. "Checking to see if I'm up to some mischief?" He wasn't at the moment, but that was going to change.

"Peter, baby," Tim said, sounding despondent. "I wish it were true." His normally giddy personality was no where to be found this morning.

"What happened?"

"How, it's shitty. Paul's been cheating on me!"

"Oh, my God!" Peter cried out. "What a bastard! What happened?" As he said this Peter was shocked to realize he had slipped his free hand down the front of his boxers.

His cock was getting hard, and he started to slowly stroke it.

Tim had started to cry. "I was cleaning out the front closet, getting ready to move some of the winter wear out of the way. Anyways, I was about to do the same to that big, puffy, blue jacket Paul wears and checked the pockets first."

He stopped and sniffled loudly.

"Go on," said Peter. He was slowly rubbing his fingers up and down the length of his cock, enjoying the growing hardness. He tried to suppress a shudder by biting a corner of his bottom lip.

Tim, oblivious, said, "I found a box of condoms in the inside pocket."

"So?"

"So?!" Tim yelled. "We've been bare-back for months. But what makes it even worse was the box was half empty!"

"What an ass-hole," Peter gasped. His hand was now moving more vigorously. What had come over him? Was it Tim's voice that was turning him on, or the fact that his friend was now technically *single*?

"Are you okay?" Tim asked. "Did I catch you at a bad time, or something?" His voice had pitched higher with annoyance.

"No! Not at all!" said Peter. "Oh, I'm sorry sweetie. This is just so much to take in all of a sudden." And with that he firmly jerked faster. He was very hot and fully erect, just the way he liked it. It took all his effort not to moan out load.

He as being so naughty! Perhaps it had to do with his long dry spell from intimacy. It had been months since he felt the flesh of another person's body on him.

Or in him.

He tried to at least sound consoling. "Have you confronted him, yet?" Stroke, stroke, stroke.

"I sent him a text a few minutes ago. Just said FOUND YOUR RUBBERS, and left it at that. Haven't heard anything back."

"Well, he probably hasn't seen it yet. Does he work on site today?" Paul was a construction supervisor, and his work in the field resulted in him missing phone calls and texts.

"Yeah, I think so. Oh, what do I do now, Peter? I'm afraid of how he'll react!"

Peter had moved his hand up to his mouth, put a finger in it and sucked. What if it was Tim's finger? What if wasn't just his finger he was sucking on?

He pulled it out of his mouth and managed to say, "Who cares now! Don't do anything else, especially when he responds. Let the cheating bastard sweat!"

This didn't really make Tim feel any better, and he started to sob. "Oh, this is horrible. I trusted him with all my heart! Now what am I going to do? I feel awful."

Peter knew exactly how to comfort his friend and make him feel amazingly better at the same time.

"Tim, honey, I want you to come over here right away. We can talk about this further. I don't want you to be all by yourself today."

"Oh, that's so kind. But don't you have work to go to?"

Peter took his wet finger and slid it down between the crack of his butt; between his firm, rounded cheeks. He started to rub himself back there. His anus tingled at the touch. Can't leave that part of him outta the fun now, could he?

"No worries, I already called in sick. Wanted to do something more constructive with my day, may as well have that be you." Tim had no clue how constructive that would be!

"Well all right. I need to get my mind off this and I think your company will help. Give me a few minutes to wash up and I'll be over soon as I can."

Peter was ecstatic. He had now slowly worked his finger inside himself. He kept it there, thrusting it in and out with small movements.

He said, "Great! Don't worry we'll work through this together. After all, what are friends for?"

He hung up, and squealed with joy. This was amazing. He had always fantasized about Tim, and now he had a chance to put those fantasies into action, with the added incentive of making his best friend feel good during a time of need.

No, not just good. *Fantastic!*

He removed his finger and smelled it. There was something strangely arousing about doing something so forbidden. Unsure with what to do with himself until Tim arrived he went to the big oak dresser and opened the bottom drawer. Inside was a myriad of exotic toys; Dildos, a vibrator, lubricant and a curl of silk rope.

He grabbed a handful of supplies, and jumped up on the bed, kicking away the covers. Won't be needing those.

Laying down, head comfortably propped up on a pillow so he could watch what he was doing, he spread his legs. He took a squeeze bottle of body oil and squirted some in his hand. It felt warm and silky.

At the foot of the bed, mounted on the wall, was a large mirror which he had positioned there for a reason. He had entertained himself with it many times, either by himself, or with company. (And with company was always the most thrilling!)

He watched himself now, from a wonderfully delicious angle. Then, with slow purpose, he began to smear the oil onto his body. Up and down his flat stomach, along the inside of his firm thighs, but staying away from ass.

At least for now!

His pectorals were muscular and he made sure to rub them over completely. He squeezed them, enjoying the feel of them. He pinched each nipple and was thrilled at getting them so erect.

Getting more excited he took the vibrator with one hand, and used his other to rub his ass-hole. He had a waxing job done earlier in the week and he loved the feel of his bare skin. Wiggling his fingers back and forth, and around his anus, he turned on the vibrator.

He ran the vibrator over his chest and pecs, feeling its mechanical sensation, and ran it around each nipple. Then he guided it slowly down his flat stomach, past his belly button, and through the small trim thatch of pubic hair.

As it touched the base of his cock he moaned.

Then his cell phone rang.

Dropping the vibrator in alarm, he was suddenly awash with a feeling of guilt. The ringing brought him back into reality. This time, the display showed it was work.

"Uh, oh," he said. Should he answer? If he didn't they might get suspicious. If he was really sick he should be home, by the phone. But if he didn't answer now, they would probably call back later, and that's when he was planning on entertaining Tim. All of Tim.

Best to deal with them now. He answered it.

Peter! You're alive." It was Abdul, his boss. "How are you feeling? Linda told me you had called in sick and thought I should check in on you, and see how you were doing."

"I'm not feeling to great, Abdul," he said. He was checking in on him, alright. But not with genuine concern. He made a pathetic attempt at sounding ill. "I hope it's only a 24 hour thing. I'd like to get back to work as we both know the work won't do itself." As opposed to him doing *himself*.

"Yeah, of course. Of course," Abdul said. "Hey, what's that sound? Is that some sort of interference?"

Peter balked. It was the vibrator! It was making its high pitched sound. He fumbled for it, but the oil on his hands made it slip out.

"Oh, that's nothing. Just the TV," he managed to grab it and flick it off. He couldn't help but feel a little disappointed.

"Look, if you need anything. Anything at all to help you feel better, just let me know. I can be over in a flash." He sounded like he was grinning from ear to ear.

Peter shuddered. Abdul was short, fat, bald, and always smelled like potatoes. And, yet, that didn't stop him from shamelessly hitting on Peter, and every other guy in the office, gay or straight. He had even groped Peter on several occasions; at the Christmas party, the Halloween party, the Thanksgiving party. Heck, anytime there was a party he'd guzzle enough alcohol to work up the courage to fondle the local help. Abdul revolted him on so many levels.

He was *definitely* not what he had in mind for today. Or ever for that matter.

But he was smart enough not to let him know that as he said: "Thanks, Abdul. That's so nice of you, but I should be able to manage." He was his boss after all, so he had to remain diplomatic, even though he made his skin crawl.

"Okay," Abdul said, sounding a little disappointed. "Well, if you need anything, just let me know." He hung up.

What I need could not be provided by him, Peter thought to himself.

With the moment of passion momentarily lost, he jumped out of bed. He stood before the mirror and admired himself. His bum stuck out just enough to be appealing, and he knew he looked great in a pair of tight jeans.

He couldn't wait until Tim saw it for himself. Maybe Peter would rub it in his friend's face for a while. They would both most certainly like that!

He smiled to himself. Boy, was Tim going to have fun today. Peter was to do everything in his power to make his best friend forget about his troubles.

There was a banging noise outside his bedroom window. Curious, he tip toed towards it and peaked through the closed curtains. Down below, beyond the fence in the other yard was his neighbour, Richard. He was busy hammering a piece of wood into the sun deck he was building.

Peter's body stiffened, and his eyes widened in admiration.

The neighbour's shirt was off, and his muscular frame was covered in a sheen of sweat. Well formed muscles rippled in the morning sun. He had a grim look of determination on his face, making him look all the more manly. Peter was intrigued, and again found his fingers where they didn't belong. Watching him work from up here got him going again.

Now *this* hunk completely eclipsed his pudgy little perverted boss.

"Well, well, well," he said. "What do we have here?"

Perhaps there was a way to kill some time before Tim's arrival, after all.

He practically skipped downstairs, through the kitchen and into the adjacent dining room. Its sliding glass door, which led to his patio, was directly across from where Richard was working. The blinds were open and his skin prickled with anticipation.

Slowly he padded across the linoleum tiles, his feet tingling with their coolness.

Peter manoeuvred himself around the dining room table and stood completely exposed at the glass. He posed seductively, hands on his hips. But Richard continued to work unaware of the naked man only a dozen, or so, feet away from him. The concentration on his work aroused Peter even more as he imagined Richard concentrating on him with the same intensity. Especially with those muscular hands.

Moments passed and still he did not look up. Peter started to feel foolish and giggled to himself. This was ridiculous. So, with determination, he rapped loudly on the glass.

Still nothing. But after another bout of knocking, Richard looked up.

Peter took this moment to smile brightly, and pose; hands upraised in a 'ta-da' like manner, almost as if he just jumped out of a big ol' birthday cake.

The reaction was almost instantaneous: Richard dropped his jaw, as well as his hammer. Eyes wide, he stood dumbfounded. Peter couldn't blame him. This was not quite what you expect to see while working on a patio in your own backyard!

Peter winked at him, then did a little seductive cat walk, parading back-and-forth to the sides of the glass.

Richard gawked, and allow himself to smile. Peter was elated. Progress! Now that he put out the hook, he just had to reel this studly fish in.

He turned around, and arched his back so his muscular rump was prominently displayed. Then, bracing his hands on the edge of the dining room table, he pressed his ass up against the pane, which felt cool on his exposed flesh and balls.

He wiggled playfully.

Glancing over his shoulder, Peter couldn't help but giggle. Apparently, it was like waving a red flag in front of a bull.

Richard was hurriedly trying to scramble over the fence while still trying to keep his hungry eyes locked on Peter sexy form. Peter laughed as Richard slipped and fell to the ground. Thankfully, the fence was quite low, or he could have hurt himself.

He stood dusting grass off of his pants, looking sheepish. Peter could tell from here that he had the desired effect on the other man. Peter curled a finger at him, in a come hither manner.

Richard obeyed, and crossed the short distance with a determined stride.

Standing before him on the other side of the glass Peter could see Richard was panting heavily. Short, sweaty hair stuck to his bare flesh, accentuating his muscles. He took a moment to appraise him and Richard indulged. When Peter had worked his gaze up Richard's body their eyes finally locked. He could see the hunger in his gaze and Peter felt the same way.

Something *great* was about to happen.

Peter leaned forward, muscular pecs flexing, and unlocked the door with a flourishing flick of a finger.

Richard opened the door and stepped inside, closing it behind him. All the while never taking his gaze off Peter. Peter backed up against the dining room table and gave him a coy expression.

He had always been attracted to Richard but, up until now, neither of them had done anything about it. Well, that was about to change in a big way.

"I saw you working out there," Peter said. He hopped up on the table with a little jump, leaned back and slowly spread his legs wide. "I thought I'd give you something else to hammer for a while. Think you have the tool for the job, Mr. Neighbour-man?"

Peter believe he did. Richard's muscular shoulders rose with his deep breathing. He stepped forward. With his callused hands he embraced Peter's arms. Peter could smell the sweat of him and he shuddered in anticipation.

They kissed passionately, his tongue eagerly seeking Peter's. Richard's strong hands caressed his thighs, his back, his butt and finally his pecs. Squeezing them he pressed his bulging pants between Peter's spread legs. Richard was most certainly happy to be there!

Richard bent down and took a nipple in his mouth, sucking and teething it gently. Peter moaned, and with his hands at the back of Richard's head, pressed him closer. He obliged and switched to the other nipple, which ached against his hot mouth.

Peter jerked himself vigorously, and now wanted much more. Pushing Richard upwards he made him wait as he slowly undid the button of Richard's jeans. Then, as he stuck out a tongue with playful concentration, Peter unzipped Richard's fly.

With several firm tugs, Peter managed to pull down his pants revealing his excitement.

"Yummy," Peter declared. He grabbed Richard's swollen shaft and hungrily took the fat prick into his mouth. He began to work it with a technique that was all his own. Richard groaned. Peter managed a smile despite the fat cock impeding the expression.

He sucked on him diligently, stroking up and down, all the while never losing him from his lips. Wet sucking noises filled the empty house, punctuated with the occasional moan from the both of them.

When he was certain Richard was close to climaxing he eased up just enough to keep the inevitable from happening. He wasn't done with them yet!

"You're not getting off that easy," Peter said. "Pun intended," he winked up at him.

Richard managed to laugh, and his breathing slowed. Peter knew he had this hunk under control. This was going better than he had hoped.

"Let's get creative," Peter said, and pushed him back a little while dropping to his knees. Richard grinned down at him like a horny teenager.

"Not what you think, big guy," he offered an evil grin. "Turn around."

Richard didn't move right away, momentarily confused as to his intent. Peter arched a brow and said, "Aren't you curious as to how freaky I can get?"

His eyes widened but he did as he was told.

Peter giggled and smacked his hairy bum. His muscular buttocks were incredibly firm and resembled the two halves of basketball.

"God, I'm a lucky guy!" Peter took a butt cheek in each hand and spread them as far as they would go, exposing his ass-hole. "And you, Mister Neighbour-man, are a very, very lucky boy."

And with that declaration he shoved his face fully into Richard's ass. Richard moaned loudly.

Slowly, Peter worked his wet, hot tongue slowly over his ass-hole, again and again. The feel of his flesh against his cheeks, and even his ears, excited him tremendously. Peter started to jerk himself off, slowly but methodically.

After a few minutes of intense and licking, and exaggerated slurping sounds for effect, Peter reached around Richard with both hands and stroked his cock. One hand gripping his length, while using the thumb of the other to rub the tip of its engorged head.

Then, with well practised technique and bold determination, he slowly worked the tip of his tongue inside him, all the while keeping Richard's ass-hole encompassed by his hungry lips.

With careful management, Peter kept him from exploding even though it felt like he could pop at any moment.

Peter felt the sweat from Richard's back trickle down, roll down his butt, and over his nose, which was firmly planted against Richard's tailbone. He managed a muffled chuckle as he thrust his tongue deeper, keeping his hot flesh pressed against his face.

"Jesus, you are a dirty boy," Richard was able to say between excited breaths. Peter wanted to give a playful response but he was too busy.

They continued like this for several minutes. Peter eventually took one hand away and slid it between Richard's muscular thighs, and grabbed his balls firmly. He kneading them gently.

Richard shuddered and shook with the intensity of their act.

When Peter was satisfied he had worked enough wonders, he put both his arms underneath him. Then he guided Richard backwards until he was above him, until he was practically straddling his up-turned face. As Richard leaned against the dining room table for balance, Peter took his balls in his mouth.

Again, he sucked, sometimes popping them out with a flourish, only to immediately take them back in again. He used his probing tongue to explore their form and move them around his mouth playfully. All the while he had a magnificent view of Richard's ass, with his nose jammed up in it. Richard reached down and squeezed Peter's nipples.

Richard trembled, and Peter moaned with the satisfaction that his neighbour right where he wanted him.

This was his way of doing things, working one part of the body for as long as was possible until the recipient was close to complete Nirvana. If anything, he was a trooper.

Because of his greedy slurping, and load moaning, Peter didn't notice Richard was trying to say something until he reached back to place a palm on Peter's forehead, indicating he should stop. Disappointed, Peter let his balls go with a wet pop of his lips. The dangled, glistening with his spit.

"What?" Peter asked while getting a good gasp of air.

"Someone is at the front door!" Richard exclaimed. Worry edged his voice.

Then Peter heard it. The doorbell!

"Oh, my God," Peter said. "It's Tim!"

How could he have forgotten about Tim so soon? Of course, seeing Richard's naked form before him explained that.

Peter jumped up. "Wait here," he commanded, and chuckled at Richard's uncertainty as he left the dining room.

"Who's Tim?" Richard called after him.

Peter ran through the house. Every inch of his skin tingled with the excitement of this sexual adventure, and heart pounded as fast as a bird's.

When he reached the door he peered through the peep hole. Tim was outside, looking distraught.

Taking a deep breath to calm his nerves Peter opened the door, but shielded his nakedness with it. He stuck his head out and said, "Tim, baby! Get in here!"

Tim was still very upset, and marched inside without even looking at him. "I'm a nervous wreck, and nearly got into two accidents on the way over. I swear I hit every red light in the city. I tell you I'm in need of very good distraction from my problems right now..."

His voice trailed off as he turned and saw Peter's naked body, which gleamed with sweat and oil. For a moment Tim said nothing and just gawked.

Unsure as to what to do Peter did his 'ta-da' pose.

"Peter!" Tim managed. To say he looked surprised was an understatement in the extreme.

"Tim!" Peter returned.

"You're.... you're buck naked!"

"And you are not," Peter said, putting his hands on his hips and giving the best pouting expression he could muster. "What do we do about this? We can't have such a disparaging difference in my house, now can we?"

"Uh..." was all Tim could say. Despite his surprise Tim's eyes continually moved over his body. Taking in each part one by one, only to repeat the cycle again. Peter suspected he was impressed, and perhaps more than a little smitten with the view.

Peter smiled. "I am spectacular, aren't I?"

Tim's mouth moved but words didn't come out at first. After a few moments of trying, and with eyes still roving, he finally asked, "What's going on?"

Peter frowned a little, and moved forward until he was standing almost nose to nose with him. He took in Tim's face with his gaze; his lips, his cheeks, his forehand, his nose, and finally settled on his deep green eyes. "What's going on is I'm going to help you forget about all your problems for the next little while. This is something I've been wanting to do to you... *with you*, for a very long time."

As Peter finished speaking he placed his arms around Tim's waist.

"I... I don't kno..." but Tim couldn't finish because Peter suddenly kissed him and deeply. They remain locked like that for several long tense moments. Then Peter felt Tim's body slowly become less rigid and finally press against his own.

Peter was pleased when he realized Tim was returning the kiss just as passionately as he was giving it.

Their tongues rolled playfully around, taking turns flicking in and out of each others mouth. Hot kissing turned to soft moans.

They used their hands to explore the others body, pressing and rubbing, with a lot of creative groping thrown in for good measure. Before Peter even realized it, he had his best friend up against the wall. One hand deftly plucked the buttons open on Tim's shirt just enough to thrust a hand inside, and clasped a pectoral. The other hand surreptitiously slipped its way down the front of Tim's pants, past the welcome thatch of his pubic hair.

With gentle firmness, and perhaps with more than a little expertise, Peter slid his fingers over Tim's cock, which was growing with excitement. Tim had grabbed Peter's ass, and pressed him against himself as a welcoming gesture.

They both groaned into the others mouth.

Caught up in the passion and heat of the moment they both began to furiously grind against each other. Eventually, between kissing, groping and chuckling, they managed to remove all of Tim's clothes.

For a moment they stopped and held each other at arms length, taking each other in. Tim's eyes were bright with excitement. "Good, God, you are one sexy boy!" he said.

Peter laughed, "And don't I know it. But you..." he said, while slowly pushing him across the living room and down into a sitting position on the couch. "You are just damn lickable."

He eased Tim back. He pushed Tim's knees back, exposing not only a luscious rump, but a beautiful nut sack, and a very tasty looking ass-hole, too. Peter gave both a quick appraising lick.

"Mmmmm," he said, like someone about to partake of a wonderful desert. "And I know just where to start."

Peter then playfully licked the ass-hole a few times, causing Tim to yelp in surprise. Peter grinned, massaging it slowly with his wet tongue, rotating over and over until Tim was quivering in ecstasy.

While he worked, Peter reached out and gently cupped each of Tim's pectorals. They were muscular, and perfectly formed, and barely moved in his grasp.

With his tongue working every contour, Peter loved having Tim's testicles pressing against his nose. Tim massaged his cock, driving himself wild.

Suddenly, Tim gasped as his eyes went wide. But not with the excitement of the moment. Peter stopped and turned to see what he was looking at.

Richard stood in the doorway of the kitchen, naked. His cock was large, and very erect. How could anyone blame him considering what he had been watching.

"Who's that?" Tim asked, his eyes firmly locked on Richard's big dick.

"Oh, that's just the neighbour. He was helping me with something earlier, and doing a fine job of it, too." Peter looked over his shoulder at Richard. "Maybe we can just pick up where we left off, huh?"

Richard was practically salivating at this point and didn't require any further coaxing. He quickly walked across the room and got on his knees behind Peter. He took a moment to run his hands over Peter's ass, smacking it several times causing him to yelp. The movement of his flesh excited Richard even more.

He licked one of his thumbs, getting it nice and wet. He then rubbed it around Peter's welcoming ass-hole.

While Richard explored him, Peter turned his attention to Tim's neglected ass-hole. Tim watched with wide eyes, mouth open in anticipation.

"I've been wanting to taste you for a very long time," Peter said, looking up at him. "So far so good. Why stop now?" Then, he gave him a nice long lick; starting from the bottom of Tim's ass-hole, then slowly up his taint, and then along the length of his cock. He ended at Tim's prick, which he then sucked in between his lips. Firmly latched on, he tickled it with the tip of his tongue.

Tim groaned, reaching down and managed to cup Peter's pecs with his hands. He massaged them over and over, feeling their hardened nipples in his palms.

Richard took his hard cock and bounced it playfully off Peter's ass several times. He watched as Peter's firm buttocks barely jiggle. Then he guided it down, and very slowly slipped the tip of it into his waiting ass-hole. Richard slid it in further. Peter paused in his vigorous sucking to gasp with the penetration, but did not remove the cock from his mouth. He quickly recovered and resumed his work.

They went at it like this for several long, wondrous minutes, and time vanished in a passionate blur. Richard pounding him from behind, while squeezing his ass. Peter licking, and sucking Tim's throbbing member, shaking it quickly from side to side while still in his mouth. Tim did his best to stay conscious, while squeezing Peter's nipples, and sometimes his own.

Richard then took control, pulling himself out of Peter. He got him to stand up, and then he guided Peter forward onto Tim, so he was now straddling Tim's face. Tim indulged them by grabbing Peter's ass and pulling him closer so his nut sack was now in his face. Peter used the top of the couch for balance, while looking down past his own erect dick at Tim's eyes, which looked up at him. The tip of Tim's nose poked up against the base of Peter's shaft.

Tim's mouth worked wonders, sucking and licking Peter's balls with enthusiasm. Peter gyrated his hips back and forth and loved the feel Tim's nose rub against his balls and taint.

Not to miss out on the fun, Richard hovered between Tim's widely outstretched legs and suddenly jammed his cock down deep inside his ass-hole. They both grunted with the roughness of the motion. Then, bracing arms on the couch where he could, he began moving his hips up and down. He pulled himself out almost the full length of his dick, until it nearly unsheathed itself from Tim, and then slamming it back down with pleasurable force. Over and over he did this, while his face was pressed up against Peter's gyrating ass, which he kissed and bit.

The house filled with the noise of their mutual love making; the near ceaseless smacking of flesh on flesh, the hungry slurping and sucking, groans, moans, the occasion incomprehensible word indicating pleasure.

Long minutes passed, until, without a word of discussion, they switched positions. This time, Richard lay on the carpeted floor, his muscular body outstretched. He smiled up at the guys. "Have a seat, gentlemen," he said.

Tim gave Peter's nuts a final sucking lick, and Peter smacked his ass as a reward.

Peter made a show of trying to pick where on Richard's body he wanted to try, then settled for his dick. He squatted over him, throwing a leg over his waist. He grabbed Richard's manhood, and pointed it up at him. Peter used Richard's prick to caress his anus, teasingly.

"You want this?" he whispered. Richard nodded. Peter grinned evilly, "You sure?"

Tim then leaned onto Richard's chest, swung his ass over Richard's face, and pushed back, sitting on him. Richard's mouth and nose were now buried in Tim's balls and ass. Richard grunted and licked.

"I think he wants this, too," Tim said.

Peter suddenly jammed down onto Richard, forcing his cock all the way insider him. Using the taught muscles of his legs, Peter moved up and down the length of him, balancing on the abs of his stomach with his hands. The quick motions, and having him deep insider his ass, nearly brought him to climax. Tim rubbed his balls and ass all over Richard's face, causing him to sometimes have trouble breathing. Richard did not complain in the least.

Peter leaned forward and kissed Tim, their mouths wide, tongues diving deeper. They played with each others pecs, squeezing, pinching and occasionally scratching at them. They took turns suckling each others nipples, tickling the tip of each with their tongues, while casting big eyes ups up at the others face.

Soon, both men started to made an effort to out grind the other, harder and harder. Faster and faster. Richard groaned with the effort of trying not to explode too soon. His face was now completely glazed with Tim's sweaty ass, and some even dribbled down through the stubble of his chin to make a tiny pool in the hollow of his throat.

Eventually the intensity caught up to him, and Richard managed to moan from inside Tim's ass, "I'm gonna cum!"

Quickly, the guys hopped off, and Richard then stood stroking, his shaft. Peter dropped down onto his knees before him. Tim joined him and they both looked up smiling expectantly.

"Yeah, alright," said Peter. "Feeding time! I'm hungry!

Tim pouted, a little. "Give me some, too!" He licked his lips for emphasis.

Knowing what they were waiting for Richard kept stroking himself while taking turns shoving his fat prick into Peter's mouth, and then Tim's. They both sucked at it until the spit dribbled from their chins. Peter even took as much of his length in as possible, causing him to gag when the cock jammed the back of his throat.

Hungry with anticipation, the grasped one another.

Finally, Richard let out a gasp, and squirt his pent-up load with a tremendous moan. He made sure both guys got an equal share, glazing their faces. They laughed as they each tried to get more. When there was nothing left to spray Richard collapsed to the floor in exhaustion.

Peter and Tim then licked each others faces, getting as much of the hot cum as they could. They then kissed passionately, exchanging their share of Richard's seed back and forth.

Peter finally sucked on Tim's chin, careful to get everything that was hanging there. Then he swallowed loudly.

Tim took a moment to slurp up what was left on Peter's face, and swallowed as well.

The men laughed at their naughtiness, and joined Richard on the floor, one on each side of him. For several long minutes they just breathed heavily, and wallowed in each others sweaty glow.

"Wow," said Tim. "That was impressive!"

"Wow," said Richard. "That was astounding!"

"Wow," said Peter. "That was fun!"

They gave each other a tired, but enthusiastic, high-five.

They all laughed.

Peter looked over at Tim, "Oh, Tim, baby, I have all these wonderful toys in the bedroom I wanted to use on you!"

Tim grinned. "I'm not going anywhere. I have the whole day to spend here. You were right, earlier, when you said you could distract me from my problems. Why on Earth would I want to leave?"

Richard chuckled. "My patio can wait until next summer, at this rate!"

Again, they laughed.

And with a smile to them both, Peter used his hands to pull them over him. He pushed at the back of their heads, guiding their mouths; one for each nipple. They both sucked, and teethed, with gusto, exchanging glances at each other across Peter's chest.

One of them (he couldn't see which, and it certainly didn't matter, anymore) caressed his dick.

Peter arched his back and moaned. It was at this moment he reached a thunderous realization:

He needed to call in sick more often!

END.

The Well Hung Hitchhiker

(His Big Fat Sausage)

Jeff faced a long, and boring drive through the countryside as he headed south to visit family for the holidays.

He found the radio annoying as it continuously played sappy love songs over and over, so he just turned off. Unfortunately, this left him with his thoughts and memories of her recently failed relationship with his ex-lover, Tom. They had been together for less than three years but he knew it had been doomed from the start. The passion that initially attracted them to each other faded quickly and they simply fell into the routine of having each other around.

And it was passion he wanted more of in his life, and since there was no more with Tom he made the painful decision of cancelling the whole thing. They separated only last month and they both knew it was definitely over. And despite being amicable it was still quite stressful.

The early morning sun gave an orange hew to the sky, and tinged the countless trees that strobe by him on both sides of the winding country road. There was very little traffic, which was why he purposely took this more scenic route to his parents house several states away. He did not mind peacefulness but having Tom around for so many years he found a lack of another person's presence daunting.

He had no one else in her life at the moment to fill the void. Neither he nor Tom were unfaithful to the other during their failing relationship. And having only just recently separated he had neither the time, nor the will to find someone.

What Jeff really craved with someone to find him. A distraction of the momentary kind. He did not think he had the emotional toolkit to deal with anything too heavy.

"I just need a man," he said to himself. He laughed at the absurdity of that declaration. He wasn't gonna find anyone at his parent's house, that was for certain. And he sure as hell didn't think anyone was waiting for him out here, in the middle of nowhere.

He peered up at the mountains, each covered with an apron of thick forest, that he slowly past by. "Nope," he said. "Only thing out here are mountain men and Bigfoot. And both would be too smelly for my taste."

As his mind wandered, he concentrated less on the road. At a particularly sharp turn, a figure suddenly appeared directly in front of him. A *man*, walking dangerously close to the edge of the road.

Jeff yelped, and yanked at the wheel, swerving to avoid him. His car fish tailed and he fought to control it. Pumping the brakes he managed to avoid flying off the road and into the trees. Always a cautious driver, he had not been travelling too fast and he skidded to a stop directly on the meridian facing the direction he had been coming from.

His fingers were dug into the steering wheel and sweat suddenly beaded on in his face. He breathed heavily.

Is that what it's like to almost die?, he thought. He barked out a laugh, still in shock.

It was only after a few moments of recovering that he realized someone was running towards the car. The stupid guy!

Oh, I'm going to tear a strip out of him!, Jeff thought as he released his vice like grip from the steering wheel, and tried to lower his heart rate with easy breathing.

His eyes widened in surprise as the man got closer. *Sweet Lord,* he thought. *This guy looks like one of those underwear models you see on bus shelter poster ads. What the heck was he doing way out here?*

Jeff found the wherewithal to roll down the window as the man ran up to his driver's side door. His stunningly handsome face was only slightly marred by his expression of concern.

"What's an underwear model doing way out here?" he blurted. He put his hand to his mouth and he gasped at his own stupidity. "Was that my outside voice?"

The man didn't seem to hear him, and said, "Are you all right? Are you hurt at all?" His voice was deep and husky. His light jacket emphasized his wide shoulders, and his jeans did little to hide his muscular thighs. For some bizarre reason his body reminded her of the trees all around, tall and strong.

Like a mountain man's!

"Yes," he finally managed to say. "I think I'm alive." Jeff grinned up at him.

The man sagged with relief, smiling for the first time, and Jeff found his perfect teeth out did the brightness of the morning sun.

"Well, that's relief," he said, placing his hands on the rolled down window. Jeff could not help but notice they were large and strong looking.

He caught himself wondering just how gentle those strong hands could be, moving up and down his body.

"I am so sorry," the man said. "It was my fault. I didn't realize I was so close to the road, I was avoiding the mud and my mind wandered."

"Oh, no, it was my fault," Jeff said. "I wasn't paying attention, my thoughts drifted..." and as he said that he realized his drifting thoughts had been about a much needed man to distract him from his troubles. He looked up at his handsome face, with its chiseled features and strong jaw. *And I go ahead and nearly kill the only man for miles!*

The man was looking at him, smiling when he had a thunderous revelation.

"Hey," he said sweetly. "Since I almost splattered you all over the road, the least I could do is offer you a ride." He felt his face reddening as he spoke, trying not make it obvious what kind of ride he really had in mind.

The handsome stranger arched a brow, considering the offer. Finally, he said, "Where are you headed?"

"South. A long way south, actually."

He frowned a little and Jeff was momentarily mortified he would lose him. But again, he regarded him with that sexy arch of the eyebrow. "I'm actually heading east, and the turnoff road I'll be taking is only a couple of miles further up ahead." He shrugged as if to suggest he really didn't want to bother him any more.

Oh, he could bother me, alright, Jeff thought.

Jeff grinned. "I'll take you to the turn off. It might keep me from running you over again when I turn around."

The man laughed. "Okay. You win. Just let me grab my backpack." He trotted away where he pack lay at the side of the road. He had obviously dropped it when he nearly hit him.

Jeff watched the movement of his buttocks in his jeans as he moved.

Yum, yum, yum, he thought.

He turned the car around in a wide arch, to point back in the southerly direction he was original travelling. This time he didn't almost kill him.

Jeff watched as he grabbed his backpack. His heart was pounding excitedly in his chest. He looked at himself in the rear view mirror, and made a vain attempt at fixing his tussled hair. He locked eyes with himself.

Do you know what you are doing, boyfriend?

He grinned. *Yes, I'm going to be doing him!*

The man came back, and threw his pack in the backseat. Then he sat down in the passenger side, closing the door. As he settled in, Jeff sneaked a peak at his crotch.

Yup, Jeff thought, *he definitely has a penis*. And a sizable one at that. With that confirmed, he now had to find out if he knew how to use it.

The man turned and smiled at him, offering his hand.

"I'm Kyle."

Jeff took it, and tried not to shiver with the electric touch of him.

"Jeff."

They shook.

Jeff found he was unwilling to release Kyle's hand right away. But when he arched that brow again and added that cute smile, he relented. He pulled out on the road and drove, trying mightily to keep his eyes from staring at him.

They made very idle chit chat, of which none involved Jeff getting naked, and Kyle spanking him. He was just trying to work up the courage to make it happen. Yet, he got the distinct sense Kyle was intrigued by him. Maybe even found him attractive.

It only took a few minutes but they arrived at his turnoff, and begrudgingly Jeff pulled over. He placed the car in park.

They smiled nervously at one another.

"Well," Kyle said. "This is me. Thanks for the lift."

He opened the door to get out.

Stop him! Jeff thought.

"Hey, what's that over there," Jeff said pointing towards what looked like the entrance to an old dirt road that disappeared into the forest.

Kyle paused and looked. "Looks like a switchback road," he said. "Runaway truck use them in an emergency."

"Wow. I've never seen one of those maybe I'll go down a little ways just to check out. Would be nice and private." Jeff looked at him meaningfully. "Care to come have an emergency with me?"

Kyle paused with the door open slightly and one foot on the road. His eyebrows had raised in surprise making him look all the more adorable.

A second passed and then another, each feeling like years to Jeff.

He chuckled slightly, then settled back in his seat and close the door. He then regarded him with a seductive smile. "That's a fantastic idea," he said.

Jeff laughed.

Hoping not to lose him in the moment, he quickly took the car out of park and steered it onto the switchback road.

Jeff drove slowly down the gravel road while fully conscious of the glances he was giving him. The moment the highway seemed a safe distance out of view, he pulled over as far as he could and parked, again.

He turned the car off, and killed the power, too, and sat back.

They both grinned nervously at each other.

"Well," Jeff said. "What do we do now?"

Kyle made a show of looking around at their surroundings. "I dunno. Is this the spot you normally take the men you almost run over?"

Jeff laughed, undid his seat belt, and moved over to him closing the distance. Placing a hand on his strong shoulder Jeff whispered in his ear, "Yes, and I would like to suck your cock, as an apology." To ensure he did not miss his meaning, he grabbed the bulge in Kyle's jeans. He was happy to note that it was already growing in size.

"Yes, sir!" Kyle said, and leaned back to undo his belt. Jeff helped him. When it was undone he eased his hips forward so Jeff would have room.

Jeff fished his dick out of its hiding place, it was firm and erect. He kissed the tip several times, feeling its throbbing heat in his hand. Gently, he started to lick its length, up and down from the base of his shaft to the swollen prick. Like a lollipop.

Kyle gasped softly, putting one hand on the back of Jeff's head to guide his up and down movements.

He then reached down, found the release for the chair and angled it back some more, giving Jeff more room to work on him properly.

With his knob glistening from his diligent licking, Jeff then took his fat prick into his mouth, pushing it up to the back of her throat as far as it would go. His lips firmly gripped his shaft as they moved closer to the base, his nose touched his stomach. Then he sucked at it, moving his head up and down all the way. He stroked him with his hand, following it with his lips.

Kyle groaned.

For several long wonderful minutes Jeff sucked his cock, until he reached a point he was certain Kyle was going to shoot his load. The car filled with sound of his hard sucking, and hungry slurping.

Carefully, he slowed, not wanting him to be spent too soon. Kissing the tip of his prick on more time, he then looked up at him with a big smile.

Jeff said, "Let's fuck."

Kyle smiled back, but offered that cute arching brow again. "It's a little crowded in here for that, don't you think?"

Jeff sat up a little and said, "Well, you are a big boy. Let's take this party outside."

And with that they jumped out of the car. Before Kyle moved around towards him Jeff pointed at him and commanded, "Strip, Mister!"

Kyle laughed, but did as he was told, stripping his clothes off, his hard on quivering with each motion.

Jeff did the same, deftly peeling off all his clothing in under a minute. They threw their clothes into the car. The gravel felt cool under his feet.

Kyle walked quickly around to Jeff's side of the car, holding onto his stiff dick.

"I want you to fuck me this way," Jeff said, motioning for him to get behind him.

Kyle stood standing with Jeff's arms braced, one against the open door, the other against the car roof. Jeff spread his legs out a little and stuck his butt out, arching his back.

Kyle smacked his ass, and moved up behind him. Holding his dick he rubbed its prick along the inside crevice of Jeff's ass, exploring and teasing him with it.

When he could no longer stand the anticipation commanded, "Fuck me! Just fuck me, dammit!"

"Okay," Kyle said, and suddenly lunged forward, jamming the entire length of him inside Jeff with one motion.

Jeff gasped, and gritted his teeth as Kyle immediately started to pound against him. His braced arms tensed with each impact. Jeff delighted in knowing that if he hadn't held himself in such a way, Kyle may very well of fucked him straight through the door with his powerful thrusts.

Kyle pounded against him, over and over, until Jeff's moans grew louder and more intense. His flesh grew red where Kyle smashed up against him. Kyle smacked his ass repeatedly, slapping each cheek in turn.

As Kyle continued to fuck him, he licked his thumb, reached around and started rubbing it over Jeff's swollen prick. He circled it with his thumb over and over.

Several minutes passed as he worked on Jeff, and the forest filled with the sounds of their passionate efforts. Jeff moaned, and occasionally yelped when Kyle smacked his reddening flesh. He gasped, trying desperately not to cum just yet.

When Kyle was close to being spent he slowed, easing in and out of him gently. He reached up and cupped Jeff's pecs, which were hard and firm. He squeezed them, and pinched at his erect nipples.

Then, Kyle pulled out of him, and smacked his ass loudly one more time.

"Ow!" Jeff cried with delight.

"I want to suck your cock," Kyle said pointing towards the hood of the car.

Jeff glowed. "Great idea!"

Jeff chuckled as he tiptoed to the front of the car. Kyle followed in hot pursuit. The hood was sloped and Jeff eased himself up it by wiggling his bum. Then he leaned back on his elbows and spread his legs.

The fibreglass popped and sagged with his weight.

"I don't think this car was designed for this," Jeff said, not caring in the least.

"Let's see what else it wasn't designed for," Kyle said with mischievous smile. He squatted in front of him, placing those strong hands against Jeff's widened thighs, then he leaned forward and gave his hard cock a nice long welcoming lick.

Then Kyle licked again, and again, until he developed a rhythm. Jeff bent his head back and smiled gloriously up at the blue morning sky, enjoying the sensation of the other man's tongue all over his dick.

Eventually, Kyle sucked on one of his fingers to get it wet, then he cautiously slipped it up inside Jeff's butt-hole, and Jeff gasped. Then Kyle started to slowly push his wet finger in and out, over and over. Jeff shivered with pleasure, practically seeing stars before his eyes with the intensity.

Kyle returned to work, now sucking Jeff's cock, concentrating more now on his swollen prick. He sucked at it, tickling it with his tongue at the same time. All the while, Jeff gasped with pleasure, squeezing pinching his own nipples. Jeff placed a hand behind Kyle's head, grabbing his hair, guiding his motions.

Kyle sucked him off for long moments, listening to the wet sounds his gyrating finger made inside him.

When Kyle had his fill he then stood, cock hard and ready. He leaned forward, so he was hovering over Jeff, and bent his dick as far as it would go. He stuck his prick into Jeff's waiting ass-hole. Jeff gasped, and grabbed onto Kyle's hips.

"You want this?" Kyle asked.

"Yes!" Jeff begged. "Fuck the hell outta me!"

And with that, Kyle suddenly slammed the entire length of his long dick deep inside him. Jeff gasped with the hard penetration. He then lifted his ass up again, so his entire dick was nearly outside him, and slammed it down again.

The hood of the car popped and squawked with the hard pressured movements.

Over and over Kyle did this, getting faster and faster. Jeff moaned with each pelvic thrust. Long wonderful minutes passed as Kyle slammed Jeff's ass again and again. Jeff's upended legs pulsated with the movements. Eventually, the intensity got to be so much Jeff's eyes rolled upwards, completely lost in the rapture of the moment.

Over and over; again and again Kyle slammed down onto him.

He could not keep up the relentless pace. With both the feeling of the rubbing wet friction inside Jeff, and seeing his face grimace with the concentrated effort of their passion, he found himself about to orgasm.

"I'm gonna cum!" Kyle finally shouted.

Quickly, Jeff pushed him back, unsheathing him from his ass.

Kyle stood before him, stroking his cock vigorously. Sitting on the edge of the hood, Jeff leaned forward so he could place the bottom of his open mouth against the base of Kyle's prick. His tongue tickled at it eagerly, and his eyes stared up at him with hunger.

Kyle stroked faster, and soon came with a loud moan. His semen spat out all over Jeff; hot squirts into his mouth which slid down her tongue and pooled at the back of his throat. Over his face in long sticky strands that splayed across his cheeks and forehead. In the corner of one eye, down his chin, and he even got some in his hair.

As Kyle sagged with completion, Jeff made a dramatic show of swallowing.

He smacked his mouth, and rolled her tongue around his lips, getting every white bit. A long thick strand still hung from his chin as she grinned widely at him.

Jeff then grabbed his dick, and sucked it as his erection faded, nursing the last of his load.

Looking up at Kyle's handsome face, seeing the sunshine glint off the sweat on his muscular chest, Jeff came to a conclusion:

He needed pick up hitchhikers more often!

END

Going Postal

(Sausage Fest)

Angus had developed the hots for the new Postman.

It wasn't lust at first sight, he wasn't really wired that way. With most men he wanted to get naked with, it took time. Like how a slow peculation leads to a good cup of coffee, his desire functioned more or less the same way.

Sort of how his current boyfriend, Dennis, got under his skin. But based on his behaviour as of late, Angus was teetering on the verge of dumping him. Especially after what he did last night at the bar. Could Angus actually cheat on him before making such a decision?

Yet, here he was, hovering near the the big bay window in his living room at the front of his house waiting for Mr. Tree-Trunks.

The previous Postman was an old, knobby kneed lech, who gave Angus the creeps each time he had to sign for a package. He always made a point of leering at Angus suggestively, and even dropped him a wink a few times. So Angus was glad for the newer, younger, and certainly non-creepy version the Postal service had decided to bless him with.

Angus had started to think of him as Mr. Tree-Trunks based on his magnificent set of legs which were as thick as, well, tree trunks; roped with very well defined muscles, and each was as wide as his own waist. As the new Postman took to wearing shorts with his uniform to fight of the summer heat, giving

Angus an eyeful each time he came to make his rounds in the neighbourhood, Angus was quite thankful for his choice.

The summer was not the only thing that was getting hot around here.

He found himself constantly envisioning those thighs pressing against the inside of his legs, keeping them wide while he pounded against him. This was more on his mind than anything to do with intimacy with Dennis. Sure, sex with him was great, but nothing spectacular. Dennis suffered from what most men did, an early finish before the race even got started. So Angus had been denied a more deep sex life than his friends did, as a result.

Did it matter that much, though? Thinking on it more, he realized it most certainly did. Maybe he needed to upgrade. Get himself into real sexual adventures, which were hindered by Dennis.

Shuddering with the thought, he decided a fresh round of coffee was needed while he maintained his vigil, and padded to the kitchen to pour one. He was wearing his morning slippers, and a robe, with nothing else underneath. Sans underwear, he felt his courage would be giving the added boost it needed to go through with what he might just do.

Him. Mr. Tree-Trunks.

Angus worked as a bartender at a gay night club. There were plenty of men that hit on him each night, some handsome, most not. Nearly all were drunk, and even rude at times. Enough so, he didn't want to consider hooking up with any of them. Besides, doing so might cause a problem if things didn't work it. Which was usually how those sort of encounters panned out.

Just look at the Dennis situation. Their relationship had slowly been unwinding almost from the start, ever since Angus began to notice the stupid things he was doing; drugs for one. Hitting on the other night club staff was another. But Angus cared about him to a certain extent. The fact Angus hooked up with him proved that, didn't it?

And, yet, Dennis never got his heart racing like the Postman did.

Impulsively, he slipped his hand under his robes, and between his legs. With an eager motion, he began to jerk himself, up and down his length, enjoying the repeated pressure against his prick. The feel of his shaved skin added to the sensation and he found he was getting hard. Very hard.

That was another boost to the courage meter: he had shaved himself everywhere this morning in the shower. He wanted to be ready, and hoped the Postman would be pleasantly surprised.

Standing in the kitchen before the window, one hand braced against the counter, the other working wonders under his robe, his face squinted in pleasurable concentration.

His masturbating grew faster, and more intense. The kitchen echoed with the fleshy sounds his movements made, and with his heavy breathing. He gasped occasionally and his grip on the counter became harder. God, he new his body well! If only he could get Mr. Tree-Trunks to get as familiar with it, too.

Okay, boy, he thought to himself, *ease up and save some for later.* But who would that later be with?

Suddenly, as if it heard him, his cell phone chimed.

Saved by the bell, he thought.

Still, he did not remove his hand. With a secret thrill he kept it there, only this time jerking very lightly, exploring his length. He walked over to the cell phone on the kitchen table and answered it with his free hand.

"Babe, you're awake," it was Dennis. Angus felt his heart sink like a stone. He was not someone he wanted to deal with at the moment. In any capacity.

Not making any effort to hide his anger with him, Angus said, "What do you want, Dennis? I don't really want to talk with you right now."

"Oh, babe," he said, soothingly. "No need to be so pissed."

He had reason to be pissed. Really, really pissed.

Last night, Dennis was at the night club while Angus worked. This had become his routine every night since they more or less became a couple. He showed up early right at opening, when few other customers would, and sat at a table right next to the server section of the bar. This way, he was always there when Angus came up to fill an order.

At first, it was kind of cute, even romantic in a way. But very quickly, when it became apparent he was going to do this each and every night Angus worked, it started to annoy him. Work only grew more crazy as the night wore on and people got more drunk, placing more orders. Having to shift his focus from what he was doing, to make the occasion comment, or chit chat with Dennis became arduous. He felt guilty when he ignored him, and Dennis seemed to feed off that.

When he asked him not come as often, he refused, saying it was for his own protection. Angus suspected he was also the jealous type, worried another man might hit on him.

Eventually, Dennis relented, but only a little. Instead of sitting at the table next to the bar, he picked a booth on the far wall, that had a better vantage point of the whole establishment. Now he could watch Angus at whatever end of the bar he went.

But this wasn't the real reason Angus was angry with him.

"You want to incriminate me further, Dennis? With you and your stupid friends?" he said.

"Hey, now," he reacted defensively. "It was nothing, and you know it. You just stood there like a good boy, and I appreciate that."

While Angus was making the drinks for a group of customers, Dennis had caught his eye by waving at him furiously. The near panic in his expression caused Angus some alarm.

He finished making the drinks, took the money for them, and departed as quickly as professionalism would allow. When he went over to Dennis' booth he found he had two of his friends sitting across from him. Angus had met them before but had made a point of forgetting their names. Low lives, the both of them.

"Angus, baby, are there any police here tonight?" Dennis had asked.

Confused, he shook his head. "No, not that I know of. Why?"

Dennis didn't answer, instead he looked over at one of his friends and said, "Coast is clear."

And with that, his friend revealed a tiny brown envelope from which he started to carefully shake out a white powder into a line in front of him on the table.

Cocaine.

Shocked and disgusted, Angus turned to leave. But Dennis grabbed his arm, in a way that was borderline aggressive. "No, babe, don't go yet."

"I don't want any!" he blurted. It wasn't what he really wanted to say, but that's what came out.

Dennis grinned at him, and he found all the handsomeness vanish from his face as he said, "No, just stand there, make sure no one can see."

Angus was incredulous, not only just with the fact he had blatantly used him to see if cops were on the premises, but also the fact he had used him as a human shield to conceal their illegal activity.

Right at that moment he knew he would never have sex with him again. As great and passionate as it was(although, always short), this was just a serious turn off.

Furious, but finding himself unable to move, he watched as both of his friends snorted up a line. And then Dennis did one, too.

The millisecond Dennis was finished, Angus whirled and marched through the crowd. He had called after him, but his voice was lost in the din. Besides, Angus had real work to do.

And now Dennis had called him, concerned. Not over having used him in such a terrible manner that Angus would feel hurt, but over the fact he didn't get away with it.

Well, he wasn't going to let him. Now Angus was actually glad he called.

"Dennis, you know, last night was a water shed for me in terms of our relationship", he said. "I think things between us are over."

"Water shed?" he said. "What does that mean?"

"As in I now know things now I wish I had known at the outset of our hooking up," he said impatiently, almost like an exasperated parent would when explaining something to a child.

"Ah, now, babe, don't be that way. It wasn't that big of a deal. I knew you were cool. You are cool, aren't you? I'm not wrong about that now, am I?"

Angus was almost rendered speechless by his attempt to make him feel guilty.

"You know what? We're done. Don't call me again, and don't you dare show up at my work either. WE ARE THROUGH!" And with that he hung up the phone. He almost wished he had one of those old rotary versions so he could slam it down.

What an ass-hole, he thought. *How dare he use me like that!*

Angus took a few moments to gather himself, taking sips of his coffee.

Well, now, he thought. *Guess this makes me technically single.*

Again, he slipped his free hand down to the hardness dangling between his thighs, rubbing his thumb on his prick. God, that felt good.

He grinned mischievously. *I wonder just how much trouble a newly single guy could get into in one morning?* He thought.

Again, as if by providence, there was another ring. But it wasn't the phone.

It was the doorbell.

He gasped with delight. Mr. Tree-Trunks was making a delivery! And just in time, too.

Skipping to the door, he remembered to synch up his robes covering up his exposed flesh. *Don't want to overwhelm the poor dear so soon,* he thought.

Without looking through the peep hole, he swung the door open. He let out a little yelp in surprise at who it was.

A handsome blonde man stood there, carrying a small suitcase.

"Angus!" the blonde yelped back. "Caught you at a bad time?"

"Paul!" Angus said,"Oh, no, I just completely forgot about our appointment." Paul was his long time friend, and accountant. They had arranged to hook up that morning for a quick look at his meagre finances, but lustful thoughts of Mr. Tree-Trunks had totally obliterated his memory.

Angus guessed that now the Postman would just have to wait for another day.

When he didn't move Paul crooked a questioning eyebrow at him. "Are you gonna let me in, or should we show off my auditing skills to the neighbours?" He smiled.

Hiding his disappointment Angus stepped back to let him past. As he did he caught a deep whiff of Paul's cologne. The enticing scent nearly knocked him off his feet. He was suddenly struck by how good that would smell up close and personal.

"The usual place?", Paul asked, and walked into the kitchen. He was wearing business-casual attire that more than complimented his manly figure. Angus would use the word hunky. That few extra pounds of muscle went to all the right places. "And I know how to use them!" Paul often declared.

Watching Paul's solid butt wiggle away from him, Angus found himself totally agreeing with that sentiment. He wondered what that butt might look like without those pants. What it looked like in action, wiggling and pressed up against his nose as he hungrily licked...

Angus shook his head. Wow! He had it real bad now, didn't he? *Still*, he thought as he closed the door and joined Paul in the kitchen, *what would it be like?* Paul was gay after all. And Paul had flirted with him on more than one occasion, particularly when they both had a few too many drinks. Such thinks were almost expected.

Paul put his suitcase on the table, and began unpacking a myriad of papers and files. He chatted, oblivious to Angus's roaming eyes, and peaked interest.

"Sorry I'm late. Had a chat with Roger that went on way too long," he flashed a smile over his shoulder at him. "Just like our relationship was." Roger was his ex-boyfriend. He ended up being just as disappointing as Dennis had been.

So, here they were, two newly single, sexy men looking for a nice healthy distraction from their ex-boyfriends. Angus' libido was now steering his brain, and he liked it where it was taking him.

Impulsively, Angus undid his robe, took a deep breath, and dropped it to the floor. He stood naked, while Paul's wonderful backside was turned to him.

Paul was still unaware. "He's such a moron, ya know? You'd figure after all the mercy sex a threw his way I could at least get him to do as I asked of him. But, nope. Men are men. Unless I was a walking television with the sports channel playing across my naval he would never have even looked at me outside of the bedroom..." Paul turned around, ready to do some business.

He froze in place when he saw Angus, standing there, looking at him with big yearning eyes, cock at the ready.

"Oh, dear," Paul said. He dropped the file folder he was holding, spilling its contents all over the tiled floor.

His eyes went up and down Angus's body, taking in every little detail, sometimes twice. Angus found this inspection thrilling.

"Uh," Paul said, "What numbers did you want me to crunch?" Always witty, he didn't even miss a beat, even when confronted with something like this.

Angus laughed, and slowly walked towards him, swaying his hips as he moved. He said, "Paul, baby. I've been thinking."

"Oh, is that how you think? Personally, I do a lot of thinking in the shower, but never considered just walking around naked..."

That was as far as he got when Angus suddenly leaned forward and kissed him full on the lips. After a few minutes of rigidness Angus felt Paul's body go loose, and was pleasantly surprised when he leaned into him, kissing him back.

Angus had put his arms around Paul's neck, and Paul, in turn, slowly eased his hand around Angus's back, just grazing the top of his naked buttocks. Their mouths opened and their tongues wrestled with one another.

Passionately, they kissed. Angus had Paul pressed up onto the edge of the kitchen table.

Skillfully, Angus found the belt buckle on his pants and undid it, all the while never losing his lock on Paul's full lips. Then as Paul eased up on the table, Angus pulled down his pants. As Paul leaned back, lifting his feet, Angus tossed the pants aside, then pulled off each shoe with a slight flourish, and a smile.

They both laughed.

Paul was not wearing any underwear, and a small thatch of trimmed pubic hair seemed to be pointing Angus to the plump cock below. It was increasing in size by the moment, seeming waving alluringly at Angus.

Angus took a moment to drink in this new view of his long time friend. Like Mr. Tree-Trunks, Paul had wonderfully muscular thighs, but lean in form. Smooth of skin, with a faint out line of a swim suit bottom.

Angus kissed one inner thigh, pressing his face deep into the flesh. Then he gently bit it, and sucked. Paul gasped, and his leg quivered. Angus turned his attention to the other thigh, choosing a succulent portion, licked it wetly several times before he bit and sucked at it as well. Paul moaned and his whole body shook. Angus enjoyed seeing the squashed form of Paul's bottom move with these sensations.

Leaning on one knee for support, the other bent to help with the angle, Angus suddenly lunged his face forward straight into the welcoming flesh between Paul's ass-cheeks. This quick acceleration of their intimacy caused Paul to gasp and buck, but he settled down to enjoy the feel of Angus's head hedged eagerly between his thighs.

Angus had as much of Paul's ass-hole covered with his mouth except for the taint where he had buried his nose against. He sucked hard and licked, making a wet sound that repeated over and over as he continued to get as much of Paul's ass-hole against his mouth.

With a loud, wet pop, he stopped, then with his fingers he lightly massaged it. Paul's anus puckered with the motion. Angus licked at it, and each time he did so he pulled back a bit, then leaned forward and licked again, then back.

Over and over he teased Paul's ass-hole.

His accountant quivered and shook, his firm flesh moving each time he did, pleasantly. Angus squeezed at one of Paul's pectorals through his shirt.

Angus then changed tactics, and thrust his tongue deeply inside Paul's ass-hole, his chin pressed in as far as it would go, his nose pressed up against Paul's nut sack. As he looked up at him, Angus' tongue wiggled up and down, exploring the inner contours of Paul's hot inner sanctum.

After several long minutes of this rousing pleasure, he slowed down, and eased his head back. A stringy line of spittle stretch out between Paul's anus and Angus' bottom lip.

Angus hungrily slurped it up.

"Oh, you are a dirty boy," Paul said, grinning down at his wet faced friend.

"You have no idea," said Angus. "I love eating ass and I'm just getting started. Let me show you what I mean."

He pushed up under Paul's thighs with his hands, rotating his butt upwards, exposing his friend's ass-hole even more.

Angus smiled, then puckered his lips and blew on it. Paul sighed with pleasure at this sensation. He continued to blow on it, watching as it clenched with each one. Then, he gave it a quick kiss. Then again, each time keeping his lips on it a little longer. Over and over he did this.

Paul smiled, and nodded. "Ah, okay. I see what you mean." He bit at his lower lip.

Angus said, "You just taste too good to stop now." He then licked Paul's ass-hole, and up his taint to include his nut sack. Paul yelped with surprise.

Another long lick, and another. Each one getting Paul's ass-hole, taint, and balls wetter and wetter with spit.

Then, on impulse, Angus shifted his hands down, clasped the curved flesh of Paul's ass and spread the cheeks apart as far as they would go, pulling his ass-hole open as far as it would go. Seizing the opportunity, Angus suddenly thrust his full tongue into the waiting gap.

"Ah, God!" Paul screamed.

Angus, caught up in the moment, poked his tongue deeper inside Paul's ass-hole, sliding it in and out, but never leaving the inside of the flesh. With his lips fully encompassing it, he sucked at the same time. He felt spit dribble from his lower lip and down his chin. Angus shook his head back and forth, forcing Paul's buttocks to slap against his cheeks.

After several long minutes of eating Paul's ass out, Angus stopped for a breather. He licked at his lips.

"You taste good all over," he said.

Paul laughed, breathing heavily.

Angus grinned, and said, "But I'm not done with you by a long shot, Mister."

Angus pointed his finger upwards, and then put it in Paul's mouth. Then he pulled it out, it glistened with spit. Angus then pointed it at Paul's ass-hole.

Paul's eyes went wide. "Uh, oh," he said.

"That a good uh oh, or bad uh oh?" asked Angus, concerned he may be about to take things to far. He didn't want to hurt his friend, quite the opposite.

"Good uh oh," Paul said. "Take it slow." The last was in a whisper.

Angus very slowly, and with the patience of an advancing glacier, slide his finger it to Paul's ass-hole, which already was slick from his licking and sucking at it.

In and out, very careful he probed his finger. Then he leaned forward again, and as he continued to massage the inside of Paul's ass-hole, he turned his attention to his neglected ball sack.

Angus slurped and sucked and licked it. The kitchen filled with the wet sounds of his mouth and Paul's moans. Occasionally, Angus wiggled his head back and forth while still clenching balls in his mouth.

Paul gripped at the back of Angus's head, pressing it hard against him. Angus reached down with his free hand and jerked off slowly.

When Paul had his fill, he gently pushed Angus back, causing him to allow Paul's nuts to pop out of his mouth. Paul shook his head and said, "No, I'm not done with you yet, either. I just want to change things up a bit."

And with that, they both stood. Paul began to unbutton his shirt, while Angus jerked both his cock, and Paul's.

Finding the buttons too small, and things not progressing fast enough, Paul just pulled it up over his head and cast it aside, revealing a muscular chest and abs so defined as to have been cut with diamonds. Large erect nipples pointed straight at Angus.

Angus grabbed at one pectoral, which was much more than a handful and latched onto its nipple. He sucked at it, while jerking Paul's cock. Then he grabbed the other pectoral, and sucked on its nipple, too.

As he did this, Paul cupped Angus's chest. They were smaller than his own, but they were lean and muscular. He squeezed and massaged them.

Suddenly, they doorbell rang.

Both men froze, looking at each other in shock.

Paul's eyes were wide with alarm. "Who is that?"

Releasing the nipple with a loud wet sucking pop, Angus gave it a quick think. It was his turn for his eyes to go wide, but not in alarm.

"Oh, I know! A special delivery, for us both!" Angus quickly bent down and scooped up his robe.

"Wait, where are you going? You're not going to answer it, are you?" Paul looked worried.

As Angus put on his robe he kissed Paul on the lips. "Trust me, this could be something very good for the both of us."

Trusting his friend, and sudden lover, Paul nodded.

"Wait here, first," Angus said as he disappeared into the living room, synching up his robe.

As he reached the door, whoever it was knocked.

Patience, patience, Angus thought to himself with a grin. He peered through the peek hole, and his heart almost stopped.

It was Mr. Tree-Trunks!

Whoa, he thought. *Could this day get any better?*

Angus took a moment to compose himself. Then, on impulse, he widened the gap of his robe to expose some slightly sweaty man muscles.

Gripping the doorknob he paused, and sniffed at the finger he had used to fuck Paul's ass-hole with. *For motivation*, he thought.

Then he opened the door.

By this time, Mr. Tree-Trunks had evidently given up waiting and had turned away to leave. But when the door opened suddenly he turned back, a pleasant customer service like smile appearing on his face. But that look froze when he saw this near naked, and slightly out of breath, hunk standing before him.

For a moment, his eyes had flashed wide. But he managed to compose himself.

"Yes?" Angus said, giving him a big pearly smile.

The Postman's eyes had glanced down at Angus' exposed muscular thighs, but quickly returned to his face. "Uh," he said. "I have a package for you."

He was holding a small parcel in one hand, and a signature tablet in the other.

Angus looked at the parcel, then up at him, and said, "Oh, I don't doubt you do. I love packages, they always have a surprise."

Again, the Postman's face froze not masking his absolute surprise. His eyes went to Angus' exposed flesh. Angus smiled at him, but also inwardly. *Gotcha*, he thought with triumph.

"Uh," he said again.

Angus laughed at his awkwardness. It made him all the more appealing.

"Maybe you could come inside, and give it to me?"

He blinked. He blinked again.

When Angus realized he was too stunned to move, he decided to keep the subterfuge going and stepped backwards, beckoning him to come in. He said, "Besides, it's to cold out. Come in and get warm. We'll work on this package of yours."

It was a warm and sunny summer day out.

Mr. Tree-Trunks, finally, got the hint. He grinned, looking at his face.

Angus grinned back, crooking a suggestive eyebrow at him.

Glancing around, as if he was worried someone on the street might be watching, he then said, "Sure, sir. I would love to give you my package."

He stepped inside, and Angus closed the door.

As he took in his surroundings, Angus looked him over. This was the first time he got a good look at him up close and personal.

Angus loved his legs, thick and incredibly muscular, like a life long soccer or rugby player. He could see their cut definition peek out at him from the ends of his pant legs of his uniform's shorts.

Taking the package and tablet from him, Angus placed them on a side table. Then he took his hand and guided him into the living room. There, Angus released his hand and walked over to the couch.

Slowly, he undid his robe and let it drop, exposing his spectacular nakedness to the second person that day.

Unlike Paul's shocked expression, Mr. Tree Trunk's was of pure appreciation.

And hunger.

Daintily, Angus sat on the couch, and leaned back, angling his butt out in front of his. He spread his legs, exposing not only his wonderfully muscular thighs, but also his well shaven ass-hole. "Care to make a special delivery in my slot?" Angus hooked an eyebrow at him, again.

The Postman did not need any further hints as to what Angus wanted to do. Quickly, he pulled off his uniform shirt, and then his shorts, revealing what Angus suspected all along (and dreamed of): a very muscular body. His torso and legs were deeply defined with muscles. He obviously was a body builder, or at the very least took good care of his body.

Very good care.

And now that body was Angus' to enjoy.

The Postman's dick was partially engorged, and roaring into a full erection with each passing second. He practically ran over to Angus. As he leaned over him, Angus grabbed the other man's cock and pulled it down to his waiting fuck hole.

"Fuck me!" Angus commanded him.

Eager to do as was told, he slowly eased himself into Angus' offered love hole, until his full length was inside him. Then, pushing Angus' legs down with his big hands, he began to thrust. Up and down. Slow at first no doubt because his brain was still trying to catch up to the exciting events that had suddenly presented themselves to him.

Then, as Angus' face contorted with the pleasure of his movements, he began to go a little faster. Angus enjoyed the feel of his muscular thighs that pounded against his ass and inner thighs, but his cock felt even better. Angus stroked himself as the other man pounded him.

For long minutes he pumped him, his ass moving up and down, hard and fast. Angus gasped and moaned with each solid thrust of his dick. He watched as Angus' flesh shook and jiggled with each movement. Angus was a sight to behold.

Careful not to lose himself too much in the moment the Postman slowed a little. Angus' eyes fluttered open and regard him appreciatively.

"Bet you didn't expect this today, did you?" Angus asked, teasingly.

"No sir," he gasped. Sweat was starting to form on his face with his hard exertions.

Angus chuckled.

Someone said, "Neither was I!"

The Postman stopped, and they both looked over to the source of the voice.

Paul stood in the kitchen doorway, his succulent naked figure outlined with the light from behind. He put a hand on his hip, and pouted for emphasis.

Angus laughed, and motioned him over. "Come here Paul, I want you to meet my new friend." He indicated the Postman, who was still leaning over him, his dick fully buried inside his ass. "Mr. Postman, this is my accountant."

"Hello, Mr. Accountant," he said, surprised yet again to be confronted with another naked man.

Paul walked over to them. "Can I get a special delivery, too? Do you have enough for the both of us?"

"Yes, sir," he said. Paul kissed him, while grabbing his sweaty ass.

Angus gently pushed him back, unsheathing his cock from him, and stood.

As the Postman and the accountant kissed each other deeply, wrestling tongues, Angus pulled a throw blanket off the couch. He spread it out over the carpeted floor, even pushing the coffee table out of the way. They were going to need the room.

Then, as the other two stopped to watch what he was doing, Angus lay down on his back on the blanket, his knees bent, feet planted on the floor.

He pointed at Paul, "Your turn to eat my ass."

He pointed at the Postman, "Paul's turn to get fucked."

Like good soldiers in the battle of pleasure, the others leaped to their assigned tasked. Paul lay on top of Angus, straddling his face with his legs, ass angled slightly upward in preparation of a special delivery. Then he hooked his arms around Angus' legs and spread his inner thighs with his hands, exposing an ass-hole waiting to be eaten.

Paul kissed Angus' anus several times, testing his taste. Paul moaned with satisfaction, as if discovering a wonderful new dessert, and began to lick it.

The Postman got down on his knees behind Paul, but not before exchanging a significant look down at Angus' upturned face.

Angus said, "I want to see you fuck him up close and personal."

He laughed, and, careful not to lean on Angus, he grabbed at Paul's muscular rump. Slowly, he eased himself into his fuck hole. Paul moaned, but never stopped licking.

Then the Postman began to pump him, watching the curvy flesh of his ass jiggle and smack against his pelvis.

Beneath them both, Angus got a good view of the Postman's cock sliding in and out of Paul, ass-hole now stretched out to take his considerable girth. His balls swung back and forth, grazing Angus's forehead with each motion.

Angus turned his head a little so he could run his tongue up and down Paul's cock without getting crushed by the Postman. Occasionally, Angus would playful pause to lick at Paul's own swinging testicles. Once or twice he managed to suck one into his mouth before the Postman's pumping action popped it out.

Several times, the Postman would pull out of Paul completely, and thrust his throbbing cock down into Angus' hungry mouth, who would suck on it hard, while tickling his fat prick with his tongue. Then the Postman would pull out of his mouth with a wet sucking noise, and jam himself back inside Paul.

Paul moaned. He was getting the most out of this little exercise, and enjoying every last second of it. He had teased Angus' anus open with his fingers, and it was his turn to stick his tongue deep inside his friend. His chin was buried in Angus' upturned nut sack. Sometimes he would lick at them, too.

Licking, slurping, smacking, and moans of immense pleasure echoed off the walls of the living room, and filled the house.

Many minutes passed like this, each participant fully lost in what they were doing. Each gaining pleasure from someone, or giving it with equal intensity.

The Postman began to moan louder, and gritted his teeth.

"Time for that delivery!" he shouted.

"Right on!" said Angus.

They all moved quickly. As the Postman stood, stroking his wet throbbing dick, the other two men got on their knees in front of him.

Angus pushed up against Paul. "Cum on his chest!"

Paul laughed, puffing his chest out, "Yeah! Get it all over!"

The Postman obliged, and while furiously stroking he let out a thunderous cry of ecstasy.

Hot jizz shot out of his cock. Gobs of sperm splattered onto Paul's pectorals, striking him in the face, too. Some ricocheted onto Angus' face causing him to laugh in delight. White sticky rivulets dribbled over his muscular pectorals, between them and down his over his abs.

After many arching squirts, the Postman, exhausted, collapsed onto the blanket on the floor.

Angus quickly began to lick Paul's chest, hungrily lapping up all the cum he could. Paul smeared cum all over him, and a small pool of cum formed in his navel.

Angus slurped that little pool up, swallowing it down. He licked everywhere there was white sticky cum. The sides of Paul's pecs, the nipples, down over his abs.

Then the guys kissed, hot cum slathering over each others mouths and chins.

When they were finished the guys laughed together. Paul smiled, then lay down over the Postman's stomach, his cum smeared chest mushed up against him, and he grabbed his sagging dick, sucking on it. He wanted all of it, and then some.

Angus laughed, looking down on his two new lovers. The day was just beginning, and there was a lot more to be done. If the Postman was spent, then he was sure Paul was now more open to doing other things.

Experimental things.

He shook his head in amazement. He did something amazing today, and knew it was just the beginning of a new sex life he had long denied himself.

Angus needed to break up with boyfriends more often!

Smiling with the thought, he joined his new lovers.

END

The Limber Librarian

(His Big Fat Sausage)

Tony loved books almost as much as he loved sex. Almost.

Yet, he never thought the two would actually collide together until he met the new handsome librarian.

He had been going to that library for many years. Occasionally, there would be an attractive librarian working there. Usually, it was someone who primarily restocked shelves with the thousands of daily returns. The work itself required lots of kneeling, stretching and bending.

When one of these cuties worked in his area, Tony found that sitting in one of the lounge chairs gave him a good view of their comings and goings. Desk cubicles, and their limiting view, where for the married, non-horny folk.

Sadly, though, there seemed to be a high turnaround at the library. Whether to internal library staff politics, general attrition (he couldn't imagine doing that type of work for years) or they were migrated to other branches, he never knew. But many hot, and/or cute, (or both) shelf restockers simply vanished from his almost weekly appreciations.

Or maybe they left because of him? He'd often wondered how obvious he was when he sneaked glances at their bums as the walked past, or bent down to add some books (That was certainly his favourite part of their job!). Also, as they were lost in the mundane concentration of their work, the almost never realized he was staring at the bulge in their crotch. Muscular pecs in tight shirts was another favourite. You may not get a full appreciation of pectorals full on, masked by a sweater or baggy blouse. But put them in a t-shirt, the pecs were particularly arousing.

Then one day, there was a new blonde librarian. He was about Tony's age, lanky in stature, but with a slim, yet very muscular figure, like a marathon runner. Thankfully, a lot of his books need restocking right in front of where Tony was sitting.

Playing casual, Tony peeked at him from over the edge of his book, thus allowing him to ogle his magnificent butt. *Jeans were created to be worn by this guy*, he thought.

He had bent over, revealing the beautiful muscular shape of his ass.

Tony felt himself getting hard, and he looked down at his crotch, making sure everything was still in order and not bulging out at a revealing angle.

"Found what you are looking for?" asked a pleasant voice.

Tony looked up, and blanched. It was him. The blonde cutie standing directly in front of him.

What did he mean? Looking for my boner? A book? Him?

"Uh," was all he could manage in that moment of shock. He became frighteningly aware of bulge growing bigger.

Did his eyes just flicker down at it? Tony thought, embarrassed. Maybe was he just looking at the book in his hand?

"Enjoying the selection?" he asked, with a crook of his eyebrow. His expression seemed to show more than a passing interest in what the answer could be.

Was he flirting with him?

"Yeah, great selection. Thanks," Tony said. *Geez, could I sound more stupid?*

"I'm Neal," he suddenly offered. "Just started here today."

Tony was a little tongue tied, not expecting to have to actually *interact* with this object of desire. *Who'd of thunk of such a concept?*

"T-Tony," he stammered. His heart was now thundering against his chest. Hopefully, his face didn't go red like it usually did when he was flustered.

"Well, T-Tony," Neal said with a smile and a wink. "Maybe I'll see you around?"

"Yeah, definitely," Tony said.

Neal turned to go, but paused. Tony's heart stopped.

He nodded his head at Tony's... crotch? At his growing hard on? He wanted to cross his legs but his erection would just make it look even funnier.

"By the way, you're reading it upside down," he grinned wickedly at him, and walked away, pushing the cart. Tony could have sworn he put in an extra bit of sway to those squared hips.

Tony watched him leave, a bit in a daze. Looking at the book in his hands, he saw that he was right.

Stunned, he waited for his hard on to die down. He even managed to read a little of the book (right side up this time), until he felt he had embarrassed himself enough for one day.

He was walking towards the exit when he suddenly heard something.

"T-Tony!" someone hissed from behind. He turned and was struck dumb when he saw that it was Neal. He was leaning around the end of a bookshelf, out of sight of the front door counter. He peeked down towards the counter then, looking back at Tony, waved his hand at him, indicating he should come over.

Thankfully, his legs took the initiative and propelled him forward, before his brain could screw things up.

When he got close, and obviously wasn't moving fast enough for Neal, he grabbed his arm and pulled him behind the shelves. His firm touch electrified his bare skin. Tony found himself grinning.

Neal grinned back. "Got a question for you, T-Tony." he said, looking quite handsome.

"Okay," was all Tony could say.

"Wanna fuck me?"

His breath caught.

Oh.

My.

God.

Tony's brain had seized up. Miraculously, he found himself nodding.

Pleased, Neal took his hand and quickly led him into a back storage room, which was filled with books, from top to bottom. He closed the door behind them.

"Now, you're going to have to wait here until closing and everyone else leaves." Neal looked up at him with big wide stunning blue eyes that melted his heart and began to stiffen his crotch again. "Will you wait here for me, T-Tony?"

Duh.

Shrugging, he said, "Yeah, no problem," he said, casually. Like getting propositioned by librarians was an everyday occurrence for him.

Neal nodded, but looked at him as if analyzing his honesty. "You know what?" he said.

"What?"

"Let me give you a little taste of what you can expect if you do stay."

Before Tony could say anything Neal dropped to his knees in front of him. Tony's eyes widened, and his boner screamed to be released.

"Whip it out," he said.

There is a God! Tony's brain seemed to cheer at him.

"Hurry," Neal said. "I'm only suppose to be on my coffee break." He looked up at him. "And I wanna little taste, too."

Tony had never unbuckled his belt, and undid his zipper, that fast before in his life. His erect dick practically popped out at Neal with the sudden motion of pulling down his pants past his waist.

Neal chuckled a little, but immediately grabbed it. The warmth of his hand on his throbbing member, nearly made Tony cum right there, but he grit his teeth.

"Mmmm," Neal said. He very gently kissed the tip of his dick. "I like the taste of that." He stuck out his tongue and flickered it against Tony's prick. He did this for several moments, alternating between kissing and flickering at it.

Then, suddenly, he opened his mouth wide and lunged forward. Nearly his entire cock was swallowed in one motion. Tony felt the top of his dick slide against the roof of his mouth, and lodge in the back of his hot throat.

Tony moaned.

"Mmmm," Neal said again. At least that's what it sounded like. He did have a big cock in his mouth, after all.

Clinching his lips around Tony's girth, he began to move his head up and down. He sucked at him, gently.

Soon, the only thing he could feel was his determined grip at the base of his shaft and part of his palm against his balls, and the hot sensation of the wonderful wet friction of his member sliding in and out of his mouth.

Tony moaned again. He was now having a heck of a time not cumming and preventing hot jizz from exploding out of the back of Neal's head.

"Neal to the front desk please! Neal to the front desk!" suddenly said a loud voice.

They both froze.

It was the intercom.

But Neal didn't lose his cool. Slowly, almost deliberately, he slide up Tony's shaft, which now was slick with spittle. His sucking lips slide over his prick, but remained locked on the very tip of it. As he looked up at him Tony felt his tongue flicker feather-like at the tip.

Then he pulled it out and gave it one last quick kiss. Neal stood, and Tony found himself standing in front of him holding his wet throbbing dick. *Was it over?*

"This is not over," he said, as if reading his thoughts. He leaned forward and kissed him on the lips.

"I liked that taste, and I'll be back for more," Neal said. "Think you can wait for me?" He grinned evilly.

"Yeah!" Tony gasped. *Sweet Lord Almighty, Yes!*

And with that, Neal slipped out the door, and closed it behind him, locking it.

Tony was left standing there, pants down to his knees, holding his dick.

Not wanting to rub one out (gotta save that for later), he did up his pants, and spent the time reading while waiting.

It didn't take long. Soon, some of the lights went off, but a bank of them stayed on in the storage room. Closing time.

Then, after what seemed like forever, the door clicked open, and for a brief moment, Tony thought someone other than Neal was going to come in and find him there.

It wasn't. Face beaming, Neal entered, and relocked the door behind him.

"Well, well, well," he said. "Tired of waiting?"

Tony sprang to his feet from the chair he had been reading in. "Nope, not at all. Uh, are we alone now?"

Neal smiled. "Yes, and let me prove it." Suddenly, in one fluid motion, he pulled off his shirt. Tony was rendered speechless, as Neal's spectacular muscular torso was presented to the world to be admired.

Tony also couldn't help but notice Neal had a six pack to die for.

"Wow," he said.

"It gets better," with a couple of quick motions, Neal pulled down his jeans, as well as his boxers, down to his ankles. A gigantic, thick dick dangled provocatively after its release. Neal grinned at him as he kicked off his shoes, and stepped out of everything, cock jiggling from its ample weight.

Eager to join in the festivities, Tony quickly pulled off his own shirt, and tossed it. Then he started on his pants but fell over onto a chair and laughed. Neal walked over to him, and put his hands on his belt buckle. Tony's eyes were on the enormous dick between Neal's well muscled thighs.

"Wait, not yet," Neal said.

Certain Tony would do as he asked, Neal sauntered over to the desk. Tony's eyes were locked on that amazingly firm butt, and the peek of the shaved ball-sack they presented.

Neal glanced back at him, then bent straight over the desk, so his elbows were leaning on the top. Wiggling his ass, Tony could now see that everything was perfectly well shaved. "I want you to spank me," Neal said.

Transfixed by the movement of Neal's naked flesh and that wondrous ass, Tony walked up behind him. Impulsively, Tony cupped his buttocks. *Sweet Nirvana!* He thought.

He wanted to fuck him so hard, right then and there, but decided to play along. Holding up a hand at the ready, he looked at Neal for his queue.

"Spank me," Neal said. So Tony did, with a light slap. First one cheek, and then the other. He really enjoyed how his firm buttocks moved when he did so.

Neal shuddered, and said, "Harder! And don't be a pussy about it!"

Well, okay then, Tony thought.

He did, this time a little harder, and using his full palm, not just the fingers. Neal yelped, and Tony found his hand actually stung.

"More!" Neal demanded.

"Yes, sir!" he said, and did so. Over and over he smacked his lovely ass, until it progressed to a full on spanking. Each time Neal yelped, or groaned. He even gritted his teeth to keep from screaming out, but that didn't last long as Tony kept at it. Smack, smack, smack.

Neal raised a hand. "Okay, okay," he panted. "Stop!"

Disappointed, Tony did. "Did I hurt you?" He hadn't wanted to have this kinky little exercise end due to him being overzealous.

"No," he said. "Not yet." Neal grinned evilly.

Tony nearly came right then and there just from that expression alone.

"Not yet?" he echoed, oblivious to the meaning, but wanting to know more, all the same.

Neal pointed to one of the carts, which was full of thick hardcovers. "Grab a classic."

Obeying, he walked over to it, feeling his own hard-on bang against the side of his thighs. Not trying to be subtle, he grabbed his dick with one hand, as he picked out a book from the cart selection with the other.

"How about this?" he asked.

Neal's panting had lessened, and he was using a hand to reach around and massage his the bright red skin of his ass. "Is it a classic?"

"Classic?" he looked. "Uh, it's about medicine or something."

Neal had moved a finger over his raw ball-sack, and he flinched with ecstasy at the painful touch. "No, not that one. Get something good, something that has meaning."

Confused at the request, but not wanting to question it for fear of putting a sudden end to this wonderful encounter, Tony picked out another book.

"The Complete Dickens Collection," he said hefting the large tome. It was thick and weight a good couple pounds.

Neal nodded with a smile, one finger teasing his asshole. "That will do. It has Dick in it."

Tony actually laughed out loud. Neal laughed, too.

Tony was not going to argue this, so he stood behind Neal, and to one side. *Fuck he looks hot*, he thought. Neal had braced his arms on the desk again, in preparation of the wonderful pain.

Tony gripped the big book with both hands, and hoisted it over one shoulder. This view accentuated the wonder curve of his buttock muscles, and Tony's boner throbbed with anticipation.

"I'd really like to fuck the hell out you right now," he admitted. He almost regretted blurting it out, but God damn this guy looked fuckable as all hell.

Neal winked at him over shoulder, "Soon. Very, very soon. But first, do this to me. I need it to get going." He smiled.

God, I am one lucky guy, he thought. His face actually hurt from grinning so much.

"Ready?" he asked.

Without saying anything, Neal faced forward again, and nodded his head vigorously. He was psyching himself up.

Neal took a deep breath. Tony took a deep breath.

He swung hard aiming at the curving muscle of his ass, directly from behind.

Neal grunted, but gritted his teeth. And Tony smacked him again, then again. Over and over.

At first, Neal kept the noise he made to a minimum, but as Tony kept spanking him with the big book, he started to get louder. Soon, he was almost shouting with each and every smack.

Neal's body would even quiver with the anticipation of each hit. But he didn't tell Tony to stop. He only flinched, making his muscular ass jiggle.

Eventually, he raised his hand again, and Tony stopped. Neal was breathing too hard from the shrieking to say anything at first. Tony lowered the book, and waited. His cock throbbed for him. He looked so damned fuckable.

"Okay, okay!" Neal was gasping. "Now get some Shakespeare!"

Was he kidding? When were they gonna fuck? Tony thought, incredulous. But he did as he was asked. When a hot, naked guy, who is bent over begging to be spanked and spanked hard, asks you to do something that turns him on even more; you did it, damn it!

Tony got it, and it was twice the size of the other. Neal's eyes widened as Tony hefted it in front of him. "Are you sure?" he asked, concerned.

"Yeah," Neal said, nodding quickly. "Do it now before I change my mind! Spank my ass with it!"

Again, Tony smacked him, again Neal shrieked with pain and delight. Tony repeated this over and over until he was certain the bright red skin on his ass was going to burst from all that punishment.

This time, Neal did not last as long as previously before he raised his hand, and Tony stopped.

Tony found his fingers actually started to hurt, where they got caught between the book and the firm flesh of his ass. He could even see they made a couple of impressions on his lovely skin. Red on red.

Neal was gasping for air, and his whole body quivered and shook. *Is he having an orgasm?* He thought.

"Okay," Neal said, gulping in air. "Drop the book and get that magnificent cock over here!" Tony did not require any further coaxing.

Bent over as he was, Neal's balls and taint offered themselves almost eagerly. Tony could see he was glistening with beaded sweat to the point where it dribbled all down his sack, and partially down his dangling dick.

Tony's mouth watered just looking at it.

"Lick me," Neal said. "I want your tongue inside me."

All right! Tony got down on his knees, lightly gripped Neal's red ass, spreading the rounded cheeks a little. Then he licked his ass-hole; nice and long at first, slowly, round and round. *What a fantastic view from here,* he thought.

Neal tasted incredible and Tony told him so. His ass-hole was sopping wet from being licked so much. Tony could feel the heat of the blood brought so close to the surface of Neal's red skin, rubbing against his cheeks and chin. He licked him for several long tasty minutes until Neal was moaning again. He could feel the wetness of his spittle all over his chin, and some dribbled a little down his throat.

Careful, he poked his tongue into the welcoming hole and it was his turn to use his tongue for flickering.

Neal arched his back, groaning. Occasionally he pushed back so Tony's face was forced deeper inside his ass, and Tony nearly went mad with the feeling of it.

Tony worked on his ass-hole like this for a long time, occasionally sucking on it while licking with his tongue. Neal's entire body shuddered and quaked. Eventually, Neal couldn't handle any more, and said, "Fuck me!"

Neal looked over his shoulder at Tony's eyes that peeked over the curvature of his ass. "Fuck me with your Dickens!"

Tony stood up, grabbed his dick (or was it Dickens?) which was now pulsating, and put his other hand on Neal's ass. Then, very slowly, he slide his prick into Neal's ass-hole. Tony bit his bottom lip because he nearly lost it right there.

Taking a moment to gather himself, he then slid his entire length into him. He gasped. Neal felt so damn good; very hot, and eager. Then he slid back his length until it was nearly out, and slammed it back in all the way. Neal grunted. He did it again. And again.

Tony pumped him hard as Neal had asked him to. He marvelled at the the bright redness of his ass, and gazed down appreciatively at how his cock stretched out his little pink ass-hole. Tony reached around and down for that massive dick and jerked at it, all the while not stopping with his rhythm. Neal's flesh jiggled, but was so firm it barely moved.

Neal tossed his head back and forth, occasionally arching his back all the way so Tony could reach around and squeeze at his nipples. At one point he pulled Neal back by the elbows so he was almost standing up straight, and slammed his ass-hole harder and harder.

Soon, after all that had happened, and with the incredible sensation of being finally inside him, Tony couldn't hold it any longer.

"Ah, fuck!" he groaned loudly.

Neal instinctively knew what this meant, reached back and gently pushed at his stomach so he eased out of his ass. His ass made wet noises as if in protest.

Spinning around, Neal dropped to his knees in front of him, and as Paul stroked his shaft, Neal slurped his dick into his hot mouth. He sucked furiously until Tony practically screamed as he came into his mouth.

Somehow Neal managed to chuckle while sucking him off. His hips bucked with his orgasm, as if he was fucking his mouth. When Tony was nearly spent, Neal swallowed loudly, never letting his cock out of his mouth. Tony sagged against the desk as he continued to nurse his load.

"Whoa," Tony said. He could feel his body was covered in sweat from such wonderful exertion.

Neal pulled his cock out of his mouth with a wet pop, and said, "Well, T-Tony. Thanks for the quickie. This really topped off my day." He smiled, cum dangling from his chin, and returned to sucking him dry.

Chuckling, Tony couldn't agree more!

END

www.ingramcontent.com/pod-product-compliance
Lightning Source LLC
Chambersburg PA
CBHW052103150726
48002CB00006B/2204